Western Christmas Magic

I0625900

The Christmas

Truce

J. L. Dawson

Western Christmas Magic

The

Christmas Truce

By J L Dawson

Butterfly Books

PUBLISHING

Cover design by: Nancy Fraser
Edited by: Sharon Dean
ISBN (Paperback) 978-1-7386019-2-9
ISBN (E-book) 978-1-7386019-1-2
A CiP catalogue record for this title is available from the National Library of New Zealand.

First edition, 2024 Butterfly Books Publishing

Contact the author or subscribe to newsletter:
jldawsonauthor@yahoo.com
www.jodawsonauthor.com

Contents

One

Constable Benjamin Kelly leaped to the ground in one bound, avoiding the stairs entirely. He pivoted on his heels and put his hand up to help the woman down.

Ellie Taylor scowled at him, avoided his hand, and pushed past him to the ground. "I don't need your help. I'm quite able to disembark from a train and find a hotel on my own." She stomped quickly away from the train, letting others dismount behind her.

Ben raised his brows, falling into step with her. "My orders are to see you settled safely to your destination, Miss. I'm to ensure your accommodations are secured and you reach Golden Oaks in one piece."

Ellie Taylor rolled her eyes and thrust her hands on her hips. "Uncle Andrew is just too overprotective."

Ben sighed and turned to her while they waited for the baggage. "Ma'am, it's common for officers to have their family members escorted to their destinations, especially a lovely young woman traveling alone. He and your father just want to see you to your destination safely. Don't resent them for it. You know as well as I do it can be dangerous for a woman alone."

Ellie twisted her mouth from side to side. She hated that he was right. A friend of hers had been attacked on a short train trip. If a Mountie hadn't intervened the outcome could've been much worse.

She sighed and gave him a resigned smile and a reluctant nod. "Alright."

Ben smiled. It was a win. She'd resisted every attempt at chivalry in their trip so far.

Ellie returned his smile and chuckled. "Thank you, Constable. You've been kind to me. I'm sorry I'm so stubborn."

Ben nodded. "I believe your stubbornness will serve you well on the frontier, Miss. It takes a strong woman to travel to a remote town on her own and make a life for herself. I admire it. Just remember that having someone help you doesn't make you weak."

Ellie chuckled. "You sound like my uncle."

"The sergeant is a smart man. He knows from experience."

"I know. He's had a tough life." Ellie gestured to two men carrying a trunk. "Over here."

Ben hurried toward the men and directed them to leave the trunk against the station wall. They nodded, relieved to be free of the heavy case.

"Stay here and I'll find us a conveyance to get to the hotel."

Ellie smiled, sat down on her trunk, and waited. She leaned back against the wall and watched the people as she thought about Ben's words. *He's right, I know the pleasure of helping others, so why do I fight him so much when he's just being kind?* She grimaced at her own silliness. *Lord, why am I so stubborn? Perhaps if I wasn't I would've accepted Jim Sowdon. He's a perfectly nice man. Father approved of him and that's probably why I didn't.* Ellie shook her head. *You'll be alone forever if you keep this up, Ellen Taylor.* She sighed loudly. Her three sisters were all happily married to good men her parents loved. "I do want that someday," Ellie whispered. "I just don't want to marry a man because he's 'a good match.' I want a man I'm wildly in love with. I don't care about position, money, or prestige. I just want a good man, who loves the Lord." She smiled at that. Her parents and sisters had long since given up on their faith when her younger brother had been killed in a bank robbery a few years earlier.

Her parents had blamed God, but Ellie had been the opposite. Davey's death had made her cling to God all the closer. Perhaps she wasn't as strong as her family. She felt so helpless without God to lean on. Her uncle had been her greatest ally. He tried to encourage his brother, Ellie's father Charles, but sadly his heart had grown hard.

She smiled as she thought of her uncle. She chaffed under his overprotectiveness, but she loved him really. He'd never married or had children of his own, and Ellie had been his favorite. They'd always been very close. It was Uncle Andrew who'd encouraged her in her nursing, despite her father being adamant that women of breeding did not go to college or get jobs.

It was Uncle Andrew who'd seen the need for a nurse at Golden Oaks advertised in the paper and arranged the trip for her. Her parents cut her off and made it clear they didn't approve. In their eyes, she was a washed-up old spinster at just twenty. All of her sisters had married at eighteen, the youngest, Erica, just three weeks prior to her trip. She'd stayed long enough for the wedding and to say goodbye to her five nieces and nephews before departing on the adventure of her life.

"Now I'm two days from Golden Oaks, and I can't wait. Lord, please help me adjust and find a home there," she whispered as Ben rode up on an NWMP wagon. "I don't suppose I'll ever see Calgary again." She sighed. "I will miss them all. I'm sure, but I know this is where God wants me to be." She spoke a little louder.

"I agree." Ben smiled. "You're well suited to nursing, Miss Taylor."

"You hardly know me?" She nodded to the two young constables who approached to help with the luggage.

"Your uncle spoke of you often. I feel like I do know you. He was sorry he couldn't make the trip with you."

"That's okay, he's busy, besides he's sent me with my very own red serge escort." She gave him a wry smile and gestured to his coat.

Ben nodded and tipped his hat to her. "At your service, ma'am."

Ellie chuckled and turned her head to look at the other two men in red serge.

Ben gestured to the first. "Constable Evan Peters and Constable James Anderton."

She nodded to them both.

Both tipped their Stetsons and said 'ma'am' in unison.

"I'm Ellie Taylor, you don't have to be so formal." She grimaced.

"It's protocol, ma'am." The younger of the two smiled at her forthrightness. Still, she was very beautiful and her eyes held a twinkle of mischievousness, so neither man begrudged helping her.

They delivered her suitcases and the heavy trunk and saw to it they were all booked on the stage for the two-day journey to Golden Oaks.

* * * *

Ben placed the case he was carrying at the foot of the bed in the suite at the small hotel. "Anything else you need?"

"No, this is just fine thank you."

"Very well. I'll come for you at seven in the morning. The stage leaves at eight."

"I'll be at the Central NWMP station. Gonna bunk in the barracks there for the night."

"Very well, I shall see you in the morning."

Ben nodded. "If you need anything, contact the front desk. They know how to get in touch with me."

Ellie chuckled and shook her head. "Uncle Andrew will be glad to know I'm being looked after."

"Just doing my job, Miss. He'll have my hide if you don't get there safely."

Ellie smiled as Ben turned toward the door. "Goodnight, Constable."

"Goodnight, Ellie."

Two

Constable Oliver Nelson placed down his axe and stood to stretch his back. He swiped his flannel sleeve across his brow and grimaced as the bank clock struck the hour. He sighed loudly and stowed his axe in the small lean-to, gathered an armload of firewood, and headed into the house. A rotund woman nodded to him as they walked inside.

"All done, Mrs. Abernathy." He dropped the wood into the basket by her stove. "I've stowed the last few piles in your lean-to, and I must get out to do my rounds." His voice was matter-of-fact rather than kind.

"Thank you, Constable. I'm much obliged."

"You're welcome, ma'am. And thank you for the baking." He gestured to the basket of cookies, cake, and bread she laid aside for him.

"Least I can do. I ain't got my boys around no more and I struggle to swing the axe these days. The Connor boys come around and 'elp me but they's out cutting trees with their Papa, won't be back for a few weeks."

"Well, I'm happy to help, Ma'am."

The older woman nodded and approached. "You know, you'd make some young woman a fine husband."

Oliver felt himself recoil and a momentary flicker of anger furrowed his brow, he exhaled loudly and shook his head. "Mounties don't have wives," he said much more gruffly than he meant to. He caught himself and exhaled. "I'll be off now, ma'am." He lifted the basket. "Much obliged."

"You're welcome, Constable."

Oliver walked to the door, placed the basket down, shrugged into this red jacket, and snatched his Stetson from the hook. He nodded to the woman and stormed out, shoved his hat on, and leaped up on Duke in a single bound. Riding with one hand holding the basket, he galloped out of town.

Mrs. Abernathy watched the man in red serge gallop away and chuckled. "You may think Mounties don't have wives, but sooner or later a young lady will catch your eye." She closed the door and turned back to her kitchen. "He's a handsome one."

Oliver slowed his horse to a walk and sighed. He wasn't fair to her. She was an elderly woman on her own and doing the best she could with no family to look after her. She didn't deserve his bitterness. Emma leaving him was not her fault, like the rest of the town, she remained ignorant of the Mountie's personal life. He liked it that way.

Here on the frontier, he could hide, start over, and get as far away from his past as possible. He kept himself busy in order to forget, but as the long summer days wound on it meant that winter would approach as it inevitably always did. Winter meant Christmas, and he despised Christmas.

He sighed loudly as he pulled up outside his office. He leaped off his horse and hurried in to stow the basket in his small quarters. Pausing for just a moment, he slipped his hand inside and swiped a cookie. Raisin, his favorite. He shoved the whole cookie in his mouth and strode back out. Glancing up the street, he observed the stagecoach pull in and managed a wry smirk. "Fashionably late as always." He hurried towards it, hoping his package from headquarters was on that stage. "I really need that camera," he muttered. His camera had been broken by a man he'd arrested, and his buddies who had pushed past him and ransacked his office a few months ago. Headquarters was just now replacing it.

He stepped aside to allow two women to pass him on the boardwalk and tipped his hat to them. Approaching the platform, he nodded to a colleague who alighted from the stage. The man returned his nod, then turned to help a young woman down.

Oliver grimaced, *wealthy and entitled.* He internally scolded himself for his presumptuous judgment of her, but he knew that type. She was clearly city-bred, her dress said as much.

The younger Mountie approached, and the young woman stood off to the side to await the luggage.

"Mountie." Oliver nodded to him. "Just passing through?"

"Yes. Name's Kelly, escorting Miss Taylor to her new home."

"Here?" Oliver frowned, the last thing he needed was to have to constantly rescue a pampered princess. *Why do they have to venture out to the prairies at all? Some kind of charitable gesture I guess, take pity on the poor folk, spread some condescension about how quaint it is, and go home for kudos for their 'bravery.'* He scoffed internally. *Well, she won't last five minutes.*

Ben smiled. "I know what you're thinking, Constable, but Miss Taylor ain't your usual rich girl."

"Huh, we'll see." Oliver eyed Ellie derisively.

Ben nodded. "My orders are to see her to the boarding house, wire her uncle, my former sergeant, then I'm headed out to my new posting."

Oliver raised one brow. "Where to?"

"Dawson City."

Oliver nodded. "Gold Country."

"Yeah, they're asking for more men, to help keep the peace."

Oliver merely nodded. He couldn't think of anything worse. "Boarding house is up the street past the mercantile. Telegraph office is directly opposite." He gestured to walk away.

"Constable." Ben stopped him.

Oliver pivoted on his heels to look at him. "You really should meet Miss Taylor, she'll be under your watch now."

"I'm not here to babysit rich girls who faint at the sight of a mouse."

"Good, because I don't need babysitting and I happen to like mice." Ellie's voice was abrupt, she thrust her hands on her hips and met Oliver's stern expression with one of her own.

"Good, because I haven't the time for damsels in distress." Oliver raised his brows and held her gaze for a moment, creasing his forehead slightly. He turned, gave Ben a nod, and strode away.

"He's charming." Ellie scowled.

"From what I understand, Nelson's had it tough. I can't really blame him. But he's a good man underneath. Worked with my brother when they were rookies."

"Well, I don't need his help anyway. I'll be just fine. I'm no delicate princess, you know."

Ben grinned. "Yes, I'm aware." He reached for one of her cases. "Now, come on, let's get you settled. I need to make Red Ridge by nightfall." At her horrified look, he continued. "But I won't go until you're settled."

Ellie hadn't meant to make that face and the feeling caught her by surprise. She was going to miss him more than she thought. He was certainly a lot nicer than that other Mountie, Constable Nelson. He was handsome, but that was all he had going for him.

Oliver seethed as he rode out of town. It occurred to him he hadn't even checked to see if his new camera had arrived. He just had to get out of there. Rich women annoyed him, and she was the very picture of the women he'd been happy to leave behind him in the city. It was part of the reason he'd moved to the frontier, to get away from their sort.

Wealthy people had made his life a misery. His mother was a maid, and he'd grown up on an estate, living in a tiny one-room cottage after his father left, leaving his mother and the four children almost penniless. The moment they were old enough the two boys had headed to the academy in search of adventure and an escape from their pathetic life. Living in the shadow of that large estate only reinforced to them how poor they were and how they'd never get out of their poverty.

It was his mother's church that had funded their way through the academy. Both he and Marty had worked hard and paid back the money they'd been given. Oliver had received a commendation and a monetary reward, which he'd given to his mother. She and his two sisters now lived in a small house on the corner of town and his mother had a good job in a store.

They were faring much better these days but still, he couldn't shake that resentment. It was only strengthened at Christmas time when the estate's opulence and wealth were clearly on display, while he and his family were lucky to find something special to eat for supper.

Oliver sighed loudly and dismounted before the McNeil household "Lord, help me with my bitterness. This isn't who Mama raised me to be," he whispered. His mind traveled back to his mother's last letter. Full of her hopes and dreams, her optimistic nature shone through every word. Unlike him, she wasn't bitter. Not even when she was little better than a slave working at the McMillan Estate. She was kind and loving to everyone, she took it all on her shoulders and never let herself be weighed down by it. It was her faith, and he knew it. He wished he could be as strong and faithful as she was.

"Pray for me, Mama, I need it. Pray I'll rely on the Lord like you do to help me with my bitterness. So many people in this world have suffered far worse than I have. I need to look forward and not dwell on the past. Lord, help me." He exhaled loudly again and knocked on the door.

Three

Mrs. Palmer, the owner of the boarding house, led Ellie to the small infirmary squeezed in between her boarding house and the post office. "This is it, ain't much but's all we 'ave."

Ellie looked around and grimaced. She turned to the older lady. "I'll make this work, thank you."

Mrs. Palmer nodded. "I gotta get back, ya need anythin' else?"

"No, thank you, Mrs. Palmer. You've been most kind."

"You don't gotta do everything on ya first day 'ere, you can rest up from a journey and start tomorra'."

Ellie gave her a sideways smile. "I came here to take care of the people of this town, and I mean to start right away."

Mrs. Palmer chuckled. "As you wish, Miss. Supper is at seven."

"Thank you." Ellie nodded and eyed the bottles and packages haphazardly arranged on the shelves. "I'll be there."

Mrs. Palmer nodded and left the room.

Ellie looked around and took a deep breath. She lifted her shoulders and dropped them again. "Alright, Lord, I'm here. I've followed Your prompting. Now, I'm really gonna need Your help." She exhaled loudly again trying to hide the growing nervousness. The task before her felt like a mountain to be climbed. With a final deep breath, she unbuttoned her sleeves and rolled them up. "Might as well get started." She grinned as a sense of God's peace that surpasses all understanding washed over her.

The small room was a mess. It was obvious that at some time a person with some medical knowledge had been there and she was pleased to see it had the basics. "I'll have to order more." She grimaced then and swiped her finger across the shelf, dislodging a large pile of dust. "Once I get this place cleaned up."

Mrs. Palmer had warned her it would need cleaning so she'd borrowed a bucket, scrubbing brush, and cleaning cloths and brought them with her.

Grateful for the hospital training that had equipped her with skills she otherwise wouldn't have, she set about cleaning and sterilizing everything.

"Miss Taylor?" A voice startled Ellie and she leapt in fright, dropping her rag just as she was leaning over the bucket. She winced as hot water splashed against her bare arm.

She stood abruptly and scowled at the Constable. "Yes?"

He folded his arms and eyed her disheveled state. Dark wisps of hair had worked loose from their pins and hung around her face. She had changed out of her gown but even her work clothes were finer than most, though now they were covered in a steady layer of dust. Her face was smudged with dirt. He turned his eyes to the room before him. Every surface was covered in bottles and bandages, packages and blankets.

He grimaced. "What are you doing in here?"

Ellie thrust her hands on her hips. "Conducting a theatre troop," she spat.

Oliver frowned and bit back at her sarcastic response. He stepped further into the room and gestured to the sparkling shelves. "I can see you're cleaning, but what I want to know is why? You've just stepped into this town and you're cleaning it, already?"

"Not the town just the infirmary."

Oliver creased his brows. "Why?"

"I wasn't aware it was illegal, Constable?" She spat at him and turned to begin lifting bottles from the small table. She carefully wiped each one, examined the label, and placed them where she wanted them.

Oliver scratched at his chin. "Miss Taylor, I'm merely inquiring as to your behavior. It's not usual that a woman of your stature would arrive in our town and begin cleaning. Forgive my impertinence but it's my job to know what's going on in my town."

She swiveled on her toes and glared at him. "Your town?"

"You know what I mean." He shrugged and tried to keep the exasperation from his voice. He knew this woman was going to be challenging. "I'm responsible for this town."

"Well, I can assure you, Constable, you are NOT responsible for me. I'm a grown woman and I don't need a babysitter."

"I'm not a babysitter, ma'am, I'm a police officer and despite what you may think and regardless of your wealth, I am responsible for you. Believe me, I don't want to be responsible for you, any more than you want me to be, but I'm the law in this town."

"And what does me cleaning my infirmary have to do with the law?"

Oliver's brows flew up and he leaned back against the doorpost. "Your infirmary?"

Ellie exhaled loudly. "Yes, you may be the law but I'm the medicine..." She chuckled at her words. "So to speak."

"Medicine?"

"I'm a nurse, Constable. That's why I'm here." She rolled her eyes as though he should've already known that, "I thought you knew I was coming."

Oliver's face grew white and his mouth dropped open. He stood up straight. "You're the nurse that we asked for?"

"Yes. What's that look for? You look like you've seen a ghost!"

"No, not a ghost exactly." He bit his lip and smirked. "It's just... I knew the nurse was coming but you aren't exactly what I was expecting." He eyed her up and down in an exaggerated fashion.

Ellie scowled and thrust her arms across her chest. "And just what were you expecting?"

"A sweet, delicate lady, someone who actually seems like they could do the job and weren't..." he gestured to her derisively "...of the manor born, Princess."

Ellie's lips trembled as if she was going to say something. Sucking back that nasty retort, she plastered on a very condescending smile. It was the best she could manage. "I was born in a manor, but I can assure you, I'm well qualified. I'd be a doctor if they'd let me but for obvious reasons..." She gestured to her skirts "... I had to be a nurse instead, but I've been involved in several surgeries and I know a lot more than the average nurse. Being from an elite family has its advantages and I got to do more than I'd traditionally be allowed. I can assure you, I am quite qualified and able to do this job." She fixed her dark eyes on his and glared deep into his soul. "So, if that makes me a princess then so be it."

Oliver was surprised to find he was actually impressed, at her strength and her ability, but he wasn't about to let her know that. She still represented everything he hated. He knew these wealthy socialites and she may be a nurse and have some skills, but deep inside she was still the pampered princess, and it was only a matter of time before something out here got the better of her and she hurried home with her tail between her legs. "That all remains to be seen. I give you a month at most. When the snows come, and we get isolated from the rest of the country, you'll be humming a different tune."

"If you say so, Constable. You're the law so you must be correct. Now if you will allow me to get back to my task. I plan to open for business tomorrow and

I have a lot to do." She batted her eyelids in exaggerated nicety.

"Sure thing, Princess. Just don't come crying to me when things get tough."

"I can assure you. I don't plan to."

Oliver shook his head and turned to hurry out.

Ellie gritted her teeth and seethed internally. "Why is he so pig-headed? Doesn't he get it? I can dress in nice clothing and still be a nurse. Being wealthy doesn't mean I don't care about people..." She paused and frowned. "Not that I'm exactly wealthy anymore." She closed her eyes. "Now that Papa has cut me off." She exhaled. *I'm going to have to be careful to get my savings to stretch. I can't guarantee these people will be able to pay me much. The council has promised free board and fifty cents a week, but can I live on that?* She shrugged. "The Lord will provide." For now, she was fine. The money she had with her seemed like plenty when she was getting a steady allowance, but now she'd have to be careful and monitor every penny. "Another new experience." She sighed and turned back to her job with vigor. "But, I do this for the Lord, and for these people, not for riches."

* * * *

Oliver strode back to his office, annoyed but unable to decide what really bothered him so much. He was actually impressed by her work ethic. She'd been in town only a few hours and hadn't wasted a moment. Still, he was certain it wouldn't last. No doubt their town was little more than a charity case to her, and she'd prove to be the pampered parlor princess he was certain she was.

He needed her to be that way, so he could keep up his prejudice and justify his hatred. But something about her unnerved him.

He both found her extremely irritating and yet interesting at the same time. He'd never known a wealthy woman to go out and get a job before, at least not a job like that, where she'd end up disheveled and up to her eyeballs in dust and dirt, sleeves rolled up and perspiration on her brow.

He snickered, as he tried to imagine the women of the estate he grew up on cleaning anything. In fact, Ellie reminded him more of his mother, that's how she looked at the end of the day. No that wasn't true, his mother was old before her time and always looked tired. He couldn't help but notice that Ellie was very beautiful, even in her disheveled state. He shook his head, forced away those thoughts, mounted his horse, and galloped out of town.

* * * *

Ellie stomped into the boarding house halfway through supper. "Sorry, I'm late, I just lost track of time." She slumped into the chair.

Confused faces turned to look at her but she ignored all the questioning eyes, giving a nod to Mrs. Palmer who placed a plate in front of her.

"Ya, look like ya bin workin' 'ard. Ya get all ya want done?"

"Yes." Ellie smiled and placed a mouthful of lukewarm potato in her mouth. She swallowed it and continued. "I'll be ready to open tomorrow."

A young man across from her nodded "What'ya openin? A confectionary?" his eyes twinkled in hope.

"No, the infirmary. I'm a nurse."

The young man placed down his fork and smiled. "Ya, really a nurse?"

"Yes, Sir. Name's Ellie Taylor, I'm from Calgary and I'm a qualified nurse."

"Name's Alvyn Tucker, Ma'am. I work at the store."

"Nice to meet you, Mr. Tucker." Ellie smiled and continued to eat her rather unappetizing meal. *Mrs. Palmer sure isn't much of a cook, but then I suppose it would've been better hot.* Ellie grimaced at her own judgmental thoughts. *That's not fair Ellie, she's not a cook, and she's doing her best. Be grateful.* Still, she'd look forward to dining at the café when she got a chance.

Mrs. Palmer paused to introduce Ellie to the eight others sitting around the table and her two children. Some were sojourners, merely passing through but five lived in the house permanently.

"So, is that why ya came 'ta Golden Oaks, to be our nurse?" Hettie Palmer asked.

"Yes, I saw an advertisement in a Calgary newspaper that you were looking for a nurse. I was surprised to find a well-stocked infirmary here."

Her younger brother nudged Hettie in the ribs. "Told ya we 'ad a nurse comin'." Alistair chided. "Ya never believe anything I say."

"Stop that you two and eat ya supper," Mrs. Palmer scolded her children.

"Yes, I came here to be your nurse."

A man two seats up from her leaned forward, he was a young man and wearing the collar of a pastor. Mrs. Palmer had introduced him as Reverend Oldfield. He smiled at her. "We had a doctor pass through a few years ago. Stayed for a few months. We had hoped he might stay long term but I think the town was too primitive for him..." He winced at all the glares he received. Hoping he hadn't said too much to put her off her and continued "...But this is a good town, full of good people."

Ellie smiled at him. "Don't worry, I have no plans to be anywhere else. This is where the Lord has led me and until He leads me elsewhere, this is where I'll stay."

The reverend smiled. "I'm glad to hear that, Miss Taylor. I take it I'll see ya at the service on Sunday?"

She smiled again and placed down her fork. "Of course, Reverend."

Four

Ellie flicked the sign to open and kicked the wedge under the open doorframe. She walked in and looked around. Grinning widely, she jumped twice and clapped. "My own clinic, how wonderful. Lord, I pray I'm up to the job."

"He'll be with ya."

Ellie spun around and frowned. "Reverend Oldfield."

"Just came by to wish ya well on ya first day. We're real glad to have you here."

Ellie smiled her thank you and observed the man. He was tall and broad, built more like a farmer or a lumberjack if she had to guess. He was in plain clothes that day and she frowned.

"Oh, I don't dress like a reverend most of the time. I took a funeral at Copper Creek yesterday, that's why I was in my suit. I spend a lot of time working with the Constable and helping my congregants. A suit wouldn't be practical for that."

"No, I suppose not." Ellie chuckled, she blushed slightly noticing his wide smile and his deep blue eyes examining her. It appeared he liked what he saw and his eyes sparkled their admiration. She returned his smile. He had deep blue eyes, a firm jaw, dark, rather scruffy hair with a short, neatly trimmed beard. He was good-looking, she supposed, but poor if she had to guess.

"Well, I just wanted to wish ya well. You got this place looking great. I can hardly wait to get sick." He raised his brows.

Ellie scrunched up her face. "That's enough of that, Reverend. Now, away with you. I need to set up my record files."

"Yes, Ma'am. I'll pray for the Lord's guidance for ya."

"I appreciate that." She gave him a genuine smile and watched as he turned on his heels and left.

She chuckled and walked over to the small desk and its pile of neat yellow folders to organize her small cabinet the way she meant to continue.

* * * *

"Good day, Constable." The reverend fell into step with the Mountie.

"Reverend." Oliver nodded his response.

"I apologize for my tardiness, I was talking to the new nurse."

Oliver shrugged. "You're not late. I was just getting to the task myself." He grimaced. "I've met the nurse."

"She's a very driven young lady," the reverend smiled.

Oliver shrugged again. "I guess."

Reverend Oldfield chuckled. "Time will tell, I suppose. Still, it's good to have a nurse in town."

"Better if we had a doctor." The Mountie tried to sound nonchalant. "Not sure I want a woman performing medicine."

"Performing? You make it sound like a play."

"You know what I mean. I never was as good with words as you."

"Well, I am college-educated." The reverend chuckled, then became serious. "What's your problem with having a woman do medicine? All nurses are women."

"Yes, but they usually work under doctors."

"Didn't pick you out to be so misogynistic?"

"Oh, I'm not, I don't have a problem with nurses in general..."

The reverend nodded knowingly. "Just this one in particular?" He raised his brows.

Oliver shrugged. "Yeah."

"You keen on her?"

Oliver stopped and scowled. "No!"

Reverend Oldfield paused and turned to look at him. "She's awful pretty, she seems dedicated to her work, and she cares about people."

"You know all that after less than a day? Sounds like you're the one who's sweet on her."

"Hardly, I don't really know her. I just think she'll fit in well around here, we really need her."

"I guess. You can be sweet on her if you want to. It's nothing to me. You know I don't ever plan to marry."

"You've told me that." The reverend got the impression he ought to change the subject. "What do you need my help with today?"

Oliver started walking again, he looked relieved at the new topic of conversation. "I want you to come with me to the Turner Homestead."

"Old Man Turner?"

"Yes, he's rebuilt his still, and I could use some help."

"What can I do, I have no authority?" the reverend asked as they entered the livery.

Oliver gestured for the reverend to help push the wagon outside. "I thought maybe he'd listen to you, he's religious after all."

The reverend shrugged. "I'm not sure what I can do, but I'm happy to try."

"Thanks, Reverend."

"You know I wish you'd call me Robert."

Oliver shrugged. "I guess I feel I should be formal when I'm doing official business." They pushed the wagon out into the sun. "Making friends can be detrimental to my job."

"That's not necessarily true." The reverend followed Oliver back into the livery to fetch the horse.

Oliver sighed. "I've seen it before, police officers getting too close to people, and emotion getting in the way of their job. Better off just keeping people at arm's length." He hitched Duke to the wagon.

"People, or women?" The reverend stood back and watched while the Mountie worked.

Oliver bent down to hitch the yoke under the horse's neck. He groaned and stood up. He fixed steely eyes on Robert. "Reverend, if I were to marry and have a family, or even develop close friendships, I'd constantly be struggling between doing my duty and being with them. And what if doing my job puts me in danger? Could I leave a widow and fatherless children? That didn't do me any good!" He gritted his teeth and scrunched up his mouth, anger flashed in his eyes.

"Constable, your father left, that's not the same as dying in service to the country. If that was the case you'd be proud of him, not angry."

Oliver wanted to scream as he fought the anger that rose in him. He hated his father for abandoning his family. He took a deep breath and just nodded. "I can't be sure I wouldn't do the same."

Robert shook his head. "You wouldn't"

"How can you know that?" Oliver shook each buckle to ensure they were tight.

"Because you know how it feels, you're a loving man. I've seen it. You can deny it all you like but I've seen you with the town's children, with the elderly women, and all the citizens. You can't fake care like that. A man with that much love in his heart needs a family."

Oliver thrust his arms across his chest and sighed loudly but said nothing. He ran his tongue over his lips, a sign of his frustration.

Robert stepped forward and gripped the Mountie's shoulder. Oliver frowned but lifted his eyes.

Robert smiled kindly. "Love will make you a better man, and a better Mountie. I promise you."

Oliver gave him a single nod and sighed. "I wish I could believe that."

"Give it time, when the right woman comes along God will give you the capacity to love." The reverend dropped his hand and smiled. "I'll pray for you."

Oliver managed a resigned smile. "I sure need the prayer." He leaped up onto the wagon.

"How are you sitting with the Lord?" The Reverend asked as he took the seat next to him.

A shrug was the Mountie's answer as he clucked to Duke, and both men sat in silence for a time. After a few minutes, Oliver sighed. "Lapsed."

Robert nodded and scratched at his short beard. "Turn back to Him. I know you carry plenty on your shoulders. He's ready to carry your burdens and walk beside ya."

"I know. I've been thinking on it."

"Well, I'm here to talk anytime you want, friend." The reverend's usual kindness laced his voice.

Oliver smirked. "We've got a forty-minute drive?"

"I'm listening." Robert immediately began to pray that no interruptions would prevent the Mountie from getting out what he needed to say and finding some healing.

Five

"Thanks for the talk, I needed that." Oliver pulled the wagon up outside the livery.

"I'll pray you find the peace you seek. Scripture and prayer are where you'll find it. Put your trust in Him and He will guide you, that's a promise!"

The Mountie nodded as they both leaped off the horse. "Thank you, I'll do my best. And thanks for your help out there. Old man Turner was far more inclined to listen to you. I pray that's the end of his moonshine enterprise for good." He bent down to unyoke the horse.

"My pleasure..." The Reverend's words were cut short by a rabbit bounding past with a wild dog hot on his heels. The horse spooked and lurched forward before Oliver could respond.

"Argh." The Mountie yanked his hand out of the way, gripping it tightly in his other hand as the claret ran down his wrist.

The horse snorted and gave him a look that could have been remorse.

Oliver grimaced and removed his other hand, a nasty gash crossed the back of it where his hand had caught in the buckle. "Just what I need." He exhaled loudly, trying to mask the pain.

"You'd better get it stitched up. I'll take care of the horse."

Oliver scrunched his face up. "I may feel more at peace now, but I can't see myself ever having an amicable relationship with that nurse."

"Love is patient and kind, remember that." Robert smiled.

Oliver raised his brows.

"I don't mean romantic love, I just mean, 'love your neighbor.' Now go, get that stitched up before your hand looks like your jacket."

Oliver nodded and glanced up at the clinic. "Might as well see if she's any good at her job."

Robert nodded and turned to the horse with a sly grin on his face. "Lord, I don't believe in matchmaking because You're the ultimate matchmaker, but a woman with some spunk like Miss Taylor would do him a world of good." He chuckled as the horse snorted as if confirming his words.

* * * *

"Excuse me, Nurse?"

Ellie looked up from her desk and frowned as she stood up. "What can I do for you, Constable? Come to give me a piece of your mind again?"

He shook his head and stepped in, holding up his hand. "Not this time, Princess." He couldn't keep the twang of spite out of his voice, despite his reverend's words. *I guess I'm a work in progress.*

Ellie glared at him. "I took an oath that I'd help people in need, all people, luckily for you, Constable." She gestured for him to sit on the bed. She hurried over to wash her hands then fetched what she needed on a small cart and wheeled it to the bedside. She picked up some powder and began to stir it into some water.

"What's that for?" he asked gripping tightly to his hand.

"For the pain."

Oliver shrugged. "No need, just stitch it."

Ellie scowled. "You don't need to be a hero, I know it hurts. Stitching the thin skin on the back of your hand is going to hurt, a lot."

"I'll be fine, it's not a large cut."

The nurse couldn't contain a growl. "First do no harm," she muttered the medical oath under her breath and grabbed his hand much more roughly than she meant to.

"Nice bedside manner, Nurse."

"Difficult patients often require a firmer approach." She didn't make eye contact as she swabbed at the wound to clean the blood off it. She paused to thread the needle.

Oliver gritted his teeth as the needle pierced his skin, it hurt more than he cared to admit. Holding his breath, he closed his eyes and thought about his mother and sisters. Trying to shut away the pain.

"Last one, Constable." Ellie's voice held a little compassion despite her growing contempt for the Mountie. "Alright, all done." She smiled and the man exhaled.

"That wasn't so bad." He grimaced, closing his hand pulled the stitches tight.

"Hold still, I'll just wrap that for you. Keep them clean and covered, if there is any redness come back and see me. They should be able to come out in a week.

Oliver nodded and managed a smile. "You did a good job." It hurt him to admit that. "How much do I owe you? Not that you need it, Princess."

Ellie sucked in a breath, fighting the snarky retort again. "Ten cents." She managed to keep her voice even and kind. Hiding behind her professional persona.

The Mountie nodded, put his hand in his pocket, pulled out several coins, placed two on the table, nodded, and walked out.

Ellie exhaled loudly and clenched both fists, she groaned. "He's so infuriating." She snatched the two nickels off the table and thrust them into her desk drawer, slamming it shut louder than she meant to.

She took a deep breath to calm herself and walked to the sink to sterilize her instruments. "Lord, give me patience and love for... ALL my patients..." she grimaced. "Even the challenging ones!"

"Excuse me." A woman stood in the doorway. Simply dressed, with a small girl clinging to her skirts.

Ellie turned to the voice and smiled as she walked to the door. "Hello. I'm Ellie Taylor. Do you need help?"

"Yes'm, I'm Caroline Elsmore, it's me girl." She gestured to the child. "She's sick."

"What's going on?" She eyed the child.

"'Er name is Annie."

Ellie knelt to smile at the child. "Hello, Annie. I'm Nurse Taylor."

The little girl gave her a brave smile. "Hello." Her voice was quiet and shy.

"Let's get her up on the table and I'll take a look."

"You did so well, Annie." Ellie smiled. She walked over and snatched the jar of candy from the shelf and held it out to the little girl. "Choose one."

The girl's face lit up and she looked at her mother. The woman nodded and Annie reached for the treat and eagerly thrust it in her mouth.

"What do you say, Annie?"

"Fank you, Nurse," the girl murmured around the sweet.

Ellie touched the girl's hair and smiled. "You're welcome. You'll be feeling better again in no time."

"In time for school?"

"Oh, I didn't know Golden Oaks had a school."

"Yes, the teacher has gone back east to visit her family, but school will be in session in a month, we hope."

"That's wonderful news. But the town doesn't have a schoolhouse?"

"The school is held in the church."

Ellie nodded. "I see." She smiled at the little girl. "Yes, I'm confident you will be well in time for school to start. It appears to be a sore throat, and it should go away in a few days with that medicine. If there is no change, please bring her back to see me."

Mrs. Elsmore smiled. "Thank you, Miss Taylor. We're awful glad you're here. Lost too many last winter, who shouldn't'a died. If we'd had someone like you here my Tommy might have lived.

Ellie gripped the woman's shoulder. "I'm so sorry. I'm not a miracle worker, and I know I won't be able to save everyone, but I'm here to take care of you all to the best of my ability and I hope I can do some good."

"You will. I'm thrilled to have a woman to take care of us. Never did feel right having to see a man for well... personal issues."

Ellie smiled. "I'm not a doctor mind, but yes I understand. It makes me feel awkward too."

"I must go, Harvey'll be expecting his supper soon." The woman gave the nurse a slightly fearful look. "How much?"

Ellie smiled. "Whatever you can manage, Ma'am."

The woman looked relieved. "Can I bring ya some of my berry preserves? I got the blue ribbon at the county fair with 'em."

Ellie nodded. "That would be lovely, Mrs. Elsmore."

"I'll have Harvey drop them by when he's in town next." The woman stopped and gave Ellie a wide smile. "I'm much obliged to you, for helping Annie."

"It's my pleasure." Ellie walked them to the door and watched them walk away. She smiled and closed her eyes as she drank in the late July sunshine. "Thank you, Lord." She felt content, more than she'd ever been before. She really felt that she was where God wanted her to be. A contented sigh escaped her.

"What's got you smiling like that?"

The voice made Ellie jump, she opened her eyes and smiled at the reverend. "Oh, hello Reverend. You startled me."

"I do apologize. You just looked so content."

"I admit that I am. I've only been here a few days but I already feel more content than I've ever been, as if I've finally found my purpose. My life's calling."

Robert smiled. "I like to hear that. It's wonderful."

"I haven't met many people yet, but I love it here."

"I might be able to remedy that."

Ellie frowned.

"I came by to invite you to a party, well not a party so much as a gathering."

"Oh, what's the occasion?"

"Sara is returning." A flicker of a smile toyed with the reverend's lips.

"Sara?"

"Sara Conway, our teacher."

Did she notice a hint of pride in his voice? She looked at him, nodding for him to continue.

"I've organized a group of us single young adults to have a meal together to welcome her home."

"At the café?"

"Yes, tomorrow evening around six?"

"Sounds fun." Ellie smiled. "Is the Mountie coming?" That brought a grimace to her face.

"I've invited him, but he seemed a little non-committal."

"Oh, well, perhaps I'll have fun anyway."

Robert chuckled and raised his brows. "You ought to give him a chance. He's had a hard life."

Ellie scowled and put one hand on her hip. "Maybe he ought to give me a chance! He seems to think I'm a pampered princess who can't do anything for myself."

Robert smiled again and stroked his beard. He fixed his blue eyes on hers. "Then perhaps you'll have to show him otherwise."

Her scowl grew wider and she thrust her arms over her chest. "If you're suggesting a romantic relationship, I'm not interested in that condescending ego-maniac." Her eyes blazed.

Robert laughed outright. "Okay, have it your way."

She snickered at her own outburst and smiled at the reverend. "I'd love to attend. It'll give me a chance to get to know more people. Perhaps I'll find a nice man, that doesn't think I'm incompetent."

Robert nodded. "Oliver doesn't think that. He told me you did a good job with his hand."

"He didn't tell me that." She sneered. "Now if there's nothing else, I must get back to cleaning up."

"No that's all I came to say. I'll see you at the boarding house."

"Absolutely, I'll be there for supper."

The reverend nodded and headed out.

Six

Ellie was just finishing her hair when there was a knock on her door. She stood and walked to open it. "Hello, Reverend."

"Miss Taylor. You look lovely tonight."

"Thank you." She gave him a wide smile and stood waiting for him to speak.

"Oh, I uh... I thought you might like to walk across to the café with me, since you don't know anyone yet." He shrugged.

"That's nice, thank you."

He nodded. "Are you ready to go?"

"Yes, I just need my shawl." She pointed to the one on the hook behind her.

Robert turned, flicked it off the hook, and passed it to her. She nodded her thanks and wrapped it around her shoulders. She shrugged. "I'm ready."

"Great, shall we go then?"

"Please, lead the way."

They strolled across the street to the café and Robert pushed the door open for her. They walked in together. A group of people were already chatting around the small tables in the corner. A buffet of food sat on a long table up the middle and a sign saying 'Welcome Home Sara' hung the length of the room.

The reverend smiled and led Ellie over to them. He walked right up to Sara and smiled. The teacher's face lit up and she blushed. "Good evening, Reverend."

"Good to have you back, Miss Conway."

"Thank you." Sara turned her eyes to the woman next to the Reverend and frowned. Uncertain if they were courting or merely acquaintances.

"Miss Conway, this is Miss Taylor, she's new to town."

"Lovely to meet you." Ellie smiled.

Sara managed a smile. "You, too." Her voice sounded unconvinced. "What brought you to town?"

"I'm a nurse."

Robert nodded. "She's reopened the infirmary."

"That's nice." Sara smiled.

"I'm glad to hear that school will be starting, too. My Uncle always said education was the most important thing and I think I agree."

All heads turned as the door opened and the Mountie walked in. Sara smiled and Ellie frowned.

Oliver walked over and stepping around Ellie, he nodded to Sara. "Miss Conway, welcome home."

"Thank you, Constable."

"I trust your trip was worthwhile?"

"Yes, thank you. My sister's wedding was beautiful. They're so happy."

The Mountie nodded and turned to Robert. "Good evening, Reverend, Miss Taylor." He managed to be as cordial as possible.

Robert smiled his response.

"Good evening, Constable." Ellie managed to keep her voice even, this wasn't the scene for an argument. She didn't want to spoil Sara's night, but she did wish he wasn't there. "I trust your hand is on the mend?"

Oliver lifted the neatly bandaged hand. "Yes, It isn't giving me any pain."

"Good," was all Ellie said. A painful silence hung over them.

Robert broke the silence. "Come on, I'll introduce you to the others." He led her to a table of young ladies.

Oliver shook his head slightly and resisted a groan. He followed Ellie with his eyes and noticed her exquisite dress. *She is very beautiful.* That thought caught him off guard and he grimaced. *Yes, she's beautiful, but that doesn't change who she is, or what she represents.* He dragged his thoughts back into line. Sara had asked him a question. "Oh, I'm sorry. Could you repeat that?" He gave her a contrite smile.

Sara stifled a grimace, she noticed the slight shine in his eyes as he watched the nurse. She smiled at him. "I was asking what you did to your hand?"

Oliver shrugged it off. "Got it caught in a buckle when my horse spooked – Miss Taylor stitched me up."

"I'm glad there's a nurse here now."

"Yes." Oliver frowned, thankful for Miss Jayne insisting they sit down for supper. He smiled and gestured for Sara to go ahead of him. He kindly pulled the chair out for her and took a seat at the end of the table.

The reverend led Ellie over and by the time everyone was seated the only chairs left were adjacent to the Mountie. Ellie scowled as she took her seat and turned her chair slightly away from him.

"Reverend would you give thanks for the food?" Miss Jayne took her seat at the end of the table.

"Certainly." Robert stood from his seat and prayed, including a thankful prayer for Sara's safe return and a blessing for the food.

All voices echoed his 'amen' and he sat back down. Miss Jayne gestured to the table of food. "Please, help yourselves."

Robert spoke up again. "Ladies first please." He gestured to Ellie. She shrugged and stood up with the other women. The men stood and waited behind them in the line.

Ellie observed the food. She turned to smile at Miss Jayne who stood behind the table. "This looks delicious."

"It wouldn't be like your city food."

Ellie sighed. "Honestly, I didn't enjoy the gourmet food sometimes. Good home cooking can be better. This all looks wonderful. Your café must be very successful." She hoped she sounded polite.

"Thank you, Miss Taylor. It was my aunt's restaurant, it's her name on it."

"Miss Dora's."

"Yes, she left it to me. She raised me from birth."

"That's wonderful. I'm glad to see there are other successful women in this town." Ellie placed a potato on her plate.

"Yes, and we're glad to have a nurse here, it's been a long time."

"I'm glad to be here, it's a lovely town."

Oliver grimaced as he walked past. "You know that having been here less than a week, do you?"

Ellie sneered at him. "I wasn't talking to you." She pivoted on her heels and marched back to the table.

The Mountie shrugged and looked at Miss Jayne. "I was just making conversation." He filled his plate and wandered slowly back to his chair. "Still alright if I sit here?" His voice held a note of contrition.

Ellie swallowed a bite of potato, looked up, and shrugged. "It's a free country, Constable, sit wherever you please. It makes no difference to me."

Robert took the seat opposite her and frowned. The reception between the two was somewhat frosty. He placed his plate down and looked from one face to the other and couldn't help but think how perfect they'd be for each other. But Oliver had made it clear that he wasn't interested. He observed her face. She was very beautiful and he admired her passionate nature. *Perhaps if she isn't interested in Oliver, she'll be willing to give me a chance.*

He turned to observe Sara. She was laughing with Lincoln McLaughlin, a young lumberjack. Her face was animated and her eyes sparkled as she laughed at a joke. Feeling eyes on her, she turned to look at the reverend, giving him a wide smile, she blushed and turned back to her conversation.

Robert smiled and observed all the faces at the table. At already nearly twenty-five he longed for a family of his own. *Lord, help me to be patient.* He hid a sigh by sipping at his coffee cup. He'd asked Miss Jayne to court but she had refused him. It hurt his pride, but he knew in his heart of hearts they weren't a good match. But to see her there with Henry Archer, her fiancé, made his heartache.

Oliver cleaned his plate and pushed it away. "I must go."

"Don't leave on my account," Ellie spat.

Oliver gave her a bemused smile. "That's quite an assumption, Miss Taylor. I can assure you, my choice to leave has nothing at all to do with you, Princess."

Ellie scowled. "Well go then. Don't let us keep you."

The constable stood. "I won't. I have to get to my rounds." He walked over and put his hand on Sara's shoulder. "I must go, Miss Conway. I'm glad you're back in town safe and sound."

Sara smiled. "I understand, duty calls, Constable."

"Yes." He flicked his eyes up at Ellie. "Not all of us can sit around and talk all day."

Ellie groaned and concentrated intently on her plate.

The Mountie farewelled all in the room, thanked Miss Jayne, and strolled out.

"That's a relief," Ellie murmured. "He was bringing down the tone of the gathering."

Robert chuckled. "I think you might've been guilty of that, too, Miss Taylor. No love lost between the two of you."

Ellie looked hurt and then saw the humor in it. She gave the pastor a sideways smile. "He brings out the worst in me. He's the most infuriating man I've ever known. Just his presence sets my teeth on edge."

Robert chuckled. "He's a good man. I hope you'll see it in time."

"I doubt it."

"Try to be amicable. The town needs you both and it's likely you'll work together from time to time. It would help if you were friends."

"Amicable, I can manage – friends? I'm not so sure. But I'm a professional and I will never let my personal feelings about a person get in the way of the greater good."

"Good for you."

"I should probably go soon. It's getting late and I want to open the clinic early. Mrs. Briar is bringing the twins by for a check-up."

"That's a good idea. We need to ensure the townspeople are as healthy as we can before the winter shuts us in. Sure will be different having a nurse here this year. We've lost too many good people needlessly in the winter months because we haven't the adequate care."

"Thanks, but I'm not a doctor."

"Still, we're fortunate to have you. You're a dedicated and clever nurse. We need you here."

"That's most kind. I'll just give my thanks to the hostess then be on my way."

"I'll walk you home."

"There's no need. I know the way. You stay and be with your friends."

"Are you sure? I don't mind. I could always come back."

Ellie smiled and put her hand on the Reverend's wrist. "I'm just fine, you stay and enjoy yourself. I'll see you at the boarding house."

"Very good." Robert stood as Ellie got up. She farewelled her new acquaintances and left the room. Robert watched her with his eyes, unaware that he was doing so. As she left, his eyes swung to Sara who was watching him, a look of confusion crossed her face for a fleeting moment, which changed to a forced smile when he caught her eye. He frowned but she quickly turned back to her conversation.

Robert stood to help himself to more food, returned to his seat, and turned to converse with Sophie and Derek, a brother and sister who lived on the edge of the settlement.

* * * *

A knock at her bedroom door caught Ellie off guard. She stood and walked to the door. "Reverend?"

"I saw your lamp was still on. Sorry if I'm disturbing you."

"No, I haven't even changed for bed yet. I got too caught up in my book." Ellie grimaced, glancing at the clock. "So much for my early night."

Robert chuckled. "I won't keep you. It's just you left your shawl behind tonight." He lifted it out to her.

"Oh." She laughed. "It got warm in there and I didn't notice."

He nodded and stood still. She looked at him in anticipation. "Was there something else?"

Robert exhaled. "I was wondering... Well, would you consider accompanying me to supper tomorrow night? Miss Jayne does a wonderful pot roast on a Friday night and I wondered if you'd like to experience it... with me?"

Ellie blushed slightly and twisted her mouth up. "Um." She thought about it for a few moments, leaving Robert to fear her refusal. "Sure, that sounds lovely."

"Really?"

"Really."

"Wow, that's wonderful." His eyes lit up. "I'll come for you at seven."

"That'll be lovely, I look forward to it."

Robert grinned. "Me too, Miss Taylor. I'll bid you goodnight now."

"Goodnight, Reverend."

He nodded and turned to hurry away. Ellie was certain on the third step he gave a little skip. She shook her head, closed the door, and headed for bed.

"I wonder if that is the suggestion of a courtship?" she said aloud as she crawled under the covers. "I don't know the customs here." She blew out the lamp. "I guess I'll find out. He's a nice man, either way, it'll be a fun night."

Seven

Ellie opened her door and smiled. "Good evening, Reverend."

Robert frowned. "Please call me Robert, tonight at least. It seems less 'congregational'. Tonight I'm not your minister, I'm just a man, taking a lovely young woman to supper."

Ellie nodded. "Thank you, Robert." She smiled nervously.

"Well, shall we go?" He smiled, equally as nervously. "I've arranged everything with Miss Jayne."

"Everything?" Ellie asked as they stepped out.

"Pre-organized our meal and our dessert and coffee."

"What do you mean by pre-organized?"

"I ordered us roast dinners, apple pie, and ice cream and coffee."

Ellie frowned. "Do I not get to choose what I want to eat?"

Robert grimaced. "Oh, I thought I was making it easier. Then we wouldn't have to waste time having to choose, we can just have our supper ready." They strode out of the boarding house onto the street.

"Are you trying to get rid of me as fast as possible?"

"No, uh, I..." The reverend chuckled nervously. "I can see how that looks, I'm sorry. I was just trying to come across as having the situation under control..."

He gave her a repentant smile. "I was trying to impress you by having everything all organized. I'm sorry. Of course, you can choose if you want to." He shuffled nervously as he opened the café door and gestured for her to walk in. *Not off to a good start, Lord, help me.*

Ellie followed Robert to the table and he seated her. Taking her shawl, he hung it over her chair behind her. "Thank you." She smiled but couldn't help thinking how awkward it felt.

Miss Jayne wandered over. "Your meals will be ready shortly, would you like coffee to begin with?"

"Oh, Miss Jayne, there's been a change of plans, Miss Taylor can choose whatever she wants. I'll cover it."

"Ohhh. I'm sorry." Miss Jayne grimaced. "I thought you wanted two roast meals."

Ellie gave her a kind smile. "It's alright, Miss Jayne. A roast meal sounds lovely." She didn't want to cause the woman more stress.

"Are you sure?" Robert fell over himself trying to make amends. "I'll pay for it, get whatever you like. Jayne, please bring us a menu so Ellie can choose."

Ellie squirmed in her chair. The awkwardness was growing. "Please, it's alright. I like roast beef and I'd be happy to have the roast meal." She gave the reverend the biggest smile she could muster. "Truly."

Jayne looked from face to face. "If you're sure?"

Ellie nodded. "I'm sure."

Oliver strode out of his office and headed in the direction of the livery. As he approached the café across the road something caught his eye. He looked up and frowned, noticing the reverend seating Miss Taylor. "What on earth?" He raised his brows and chuckled. "That can't possibly end well." He sneered. "That's quite a woman you've chosen, Reverend. Good luck with that." He paused for just a minute as a spike of some emotion washed over him. *Jealousy? No, couldn't be. I'm certainly not interested in a woman like that.* He attempted to convince himself. *There is no place in my life for a wife and family.*

Ellie pushed the rather bland roast meal around on her plate. Perhaps life in the city had meant she was exposed to food with more flavor and variety. It wasn't terrible, in fact, Miss Jayne was a good cook, and the meal was home cooking as it should be. It just wasn't what Ellie was used to.

"Everything alright? You've hardly eaten a thing?" Robert asked, laying his knife and fork on his own clean plate.

"Yes, it's just that I'm used to very different food from the city."

"You didn't like it?" Jayne stepped up, the hurt in her voice evidenced her pride in her food.

"I like it plenty, Miss Jayne, you're a fine cook, it's me, really. I'm just used to food with... different flavors to what you use. We had restaurants in Calgary with flavors from all over the world."

"Oh. I'm sorry." Jayne reached for her almost full plate and sighed. "I do the best I can with what I have available."

Ellie gripped the woman's wrist. "Please don't take it personally, Miss Jayne. Your food is very good. It's just different than what I'm used to."

Jayne nodded and blinked back the threatening tears. "I'll get your desserts." She mumbled.

"Sorry," Robert managed. "I should have thought and let you choose."

"I don't know that it would have made a difference. We had a French and a Spanish cook in our home over the years and Papa loved to take us out to restaurants to experience foods from exotic lands."

Robert grimaced. "The frontier must seem awful primitive and quaint to someone who's lived the life of a princess."

A loud gasp came from Ellie. "Princess?" The hurt was evident in her voice.

"I just mean compared to our primitive lives, your life seems like royalty."

Ellie nodded and blinked back tears. "I came here to get away from that life. I love it here, Reverend. It's just taking me time to adjust. I'm sorry if that makes me a princess in everyone's mind." Her lips trembled, and she lowered her eyes. "I would never have condemned someone from the prairies who found it hard to adjust to life in a manor house. Now, if you don't mind, I think I'd like to go and catch up on some reading." She stood, snatched her shawl from her chair, and marched out the door.

Oliver was on edge that evening. He left the livery and strode back towards his office. He was certain he'd forgotten something, or at least that's what he told himself. In reality, he wanted to know what was happening in that café. He made his third pass at the large window and grimaced as he noticed Ellie stand up, clearly agitated, snatch up her shawl, and storm out.

She looked up and caught the Mountie's eye, scowled at him, and stormed across the street to the boarding house.

Robert walked out, at a much more leisurely pace, with a look of defeat on his face. Noticing Oliver watching he gave the Mountie a wry smirk.

"What was that all about?"

"I blew it." The reverend chuckled and ran his fingers through his hair.

Oliver grimaced. "Why were you having supper with her?"

"Why does a man usually have supper with a woman?"

"You're courting?"

"No. But I was kinda hoping to see if there was a future for us."

"And?"

"It did not go well from the beginning. I presumed too many things, ordered for her, and well, I suggested she was used to a much more lavish lifestyle."

"She is rather a pampered princess." The Mountie shook his head. "I'm not surprised, to storm out like that..."

Robert raised his hand. "That is entirely on me."

"So, what now?"

"I was going to apologize."

"No, I mean are you going to keep pursuing her?" *What was that gulp in my throat? Why am I worried he might say yes? I'm not interested in having a wife or family.* But that thought was beginning to soften in his mind.

"No. I don't think so. From the beginning, it was obvious we aren't compatible. It was nothing but awkward and when she called me 'Reverend' rather than Robert, I knew we couldn't get past that."

"Oh." Oliver was not ready for the wave of relief that washed through him.

"It's alright, truly. I think she's too independent for me. It's best we remain, Reverend and congregant and keep it at that."

"Probably a good idea." There was a slight twitch to the Mountie's lips.

Robert raised his brows. "You know, she'd be the ideal woman for you."

Oliver scrunched his face up in an exaggerated fashion. "No, you know I don't have room in my life for a family."

Robert patted his back. "We'll see about that. You know, it's not good for man to be alone. We were designed by God to marry and have families."

"Yeah, I do know that. But I'm just not sure the life of a Mountie leaves room for a family. It wouldn't be fair to them. I'm gone all the time and I'm often in danger..."

Robert crossed his arms and tilted his head, squinting at the Mountie. "When was the last time you were in danger?"

Oliver nodded. "Well alright, not often around here, but the time will come, and I'm just not sure I could let a woman go through that."

"You know." Robert smirked. "I know a thing or two about women..." Both men laughed outright but the reverend continued. "I've learned that making decisions for them without consulting them is genuinely not a good idea."

Oliver nodded.

"So, why don't you worry about that when you find a lady to love, and then let her make the choice."

"Like you did?" Oliver gestured to the boarding house.

Robert chuckled. "I think I've learned a little something from this situation."

"Yeah, like maybe I'm just better off, because I don't plan to get tangled up with a woman. Even if I wanted a family, it doesn't seem worth it. Getting ya heart trampled on like that isn't exactly pleasant."

Robert scratched at his short beard. "Yeah, but being human means we are going to be hurt sometimes, and that we are going to be the ones hurting others at times. It's sad but it's inevitable. I'm not going to deprive myself of happiness just because there's a risk of being hurt. The thought of loving and being that committed to a woman and a family is wonderful. I'd hate to see you miss out on that."

Oliver shrugged. "Yeah, I guess."

Robert nodded. "Well, I best go talk to Miss Taylor. I need to eat some humble pie."

"Alright, all the best. I don't envy you that at all."

"I'll see you on Sunday."

"I'll be there."

*   *   *   *

"Ladies and Gentlemen, before we leave the service today, I want to let you know about this year's end-of-summer event."

Murmurs traveled around the congregation. Ellie looked around and shrugged hoping all would become clear. A voice from the row behind spoke. "Every year we have a town event before the winter sets in. Something to boost everyone's spirits before the snows come. The reverend started it, and it's become a tradition."

Ellie scowled at Oliver. "I didn't ask."

"You're welcome," he whispered and shook his head. They both stopped to listen to Robert.

"This year, the town council has organized a town scavenger hunt. I did one at seminary college and it was lots of fun. There will be a list of clues that each leads to the next clue. The first team across the finish line will win." Robert watched as faces lit up and nods and murmurs traveled through the crowd. "Teams will be two people and if you don't have a partner we can draw names and make up random pairings. It'll commence tomorrow at exactly 2 pm. All the businesses are on board and we have unanimously agreed to close them for the afternoon, so everyone can be involved. Meet on the town common under the twin furs for your first clue and to organize the teams."

"Is there a prize?" Hector Cartwright called out.

"Yes, of course. There will be a ten-dollar prize, and the winning team will also receive a free supper at Miss Jayne's café." The reverend smiled.

"What's the entry fee?" another called.

"There is no fee, the town council has donated the money for this event. If you wish to make a donation please feel free but it doesn't cost anything. I'll see you all there tomorrow."

"Sounds fun." Ellie grinned.

Oliver shrugged. "I guess."

Ellie hurried out and chased down Sara. "Hey, I'm excited about the Scavenger hunt."

"Uhuh." Was the teacher's non-committal response.

"Sara?" Ellie put a hand out to her. "Is everything alright?"

"As if you don't know," the teacher spat and tried to walk away.

Ellie chased her down and gripped her arm. "Sara, please. Talk to me, what's going on?"

"I saw you." Sara's voice trembled and she tucked her lips under and swiped at her eyes.

"Saw me? Doing what?"

Sara took a deep breath... "Are you and Robert courting."

Ellie frowned and tilted her head to the side. She smiled and gripped Sara's hand. "No, we are not courting."

"But I saw you, at supper."

"What you saw was the worst first date in history. It didn't go well from the start."

Sara's eyes widened and hope filled her countenance. "Really?"

Ellie grinned. "Really." She squinted at her new friend. "You love him don't you."

Sara's cheeks reddened and she nodded. "Please don't tell him."

"I won't, but you should."

Sara gasped. "I can't do that. Women don't declare their love for men."

"Why not?"

"It's just not done."

"So you're just gonna stand around and hope he notices you?"

"What other choice do I have?"

"Make him notice you." Ellie grinned.

Sara's eyes grew wide. "What are you suggesting?"

"Nothing inappropriate. I don't believe in women flirting with men, but it can't hurt to be where he can notice you." Ellie smiled. "Starting with the scavenger hunt."

"But how?"

"Remember the Reverend wants to participate so Mr. Archer and the town council will be organizing it, and organizing the teams. Why don't you go speak with the Mayor and see if he can't make sure you and the Reverend are a team."

"Isn't that cheating?"

"No, the reverend said we could have pre-organized teams."

Sara smiled. "All right, it couldn't hurt, could it?"

"Nope, it couldn't hurt." Ellie smiled. She became serious then. "I'm sorry that our supper upset you. Please know there is nothing between us. We talked and neither of us wanted more than a friendship."

"That's alright." Sara smiled. "I was just jealous of you." She noticed the mayor and his wife walking out of the church. "Well, I better go, I want to talk to Mayor Archer." She grinned.

"Good for you. I hope it works out." Ellie smiled.

"Me too." Sara gushed. She'd never done anything so bold in all her days.

Eight

"Welcome everyone." Mayor Archer spoke loudly. "We'll provide you with your first clue in just a moment but first, the teams will be as follows..."

The mayor read out the names of those who had pre-arranged their teams, then continued to those who he had paired up. "Reverend Oldfield... and Sara Conway."

Ellie noticed Sara's face light up and she raised her brows at her friend. The Reverend looked across at Sara and nodded kindly.

The names continued as Ellie anxiously waited for her name. At last, he read, "and finally Ellen Taylor and Constable Oliver Nelson."

Ellie closed her eyes and exhaled. She shook her head and groaned. "What?" She pivoted around and scowled at the Constable. "Did you put them up to this?"

"Are you kidding? I didn't even want to do this until the reverend begged me, said there was an odd number and he needed me. If I'd known I'd be paired up with a princess I would've refused." He sneered.

"Well, I don't want to be with you, either."

"Look at this." The reverend walked up with Sara. "What a team."

Oliver scowled and Ellie pursed her lips. She exhaled loudly. "I think you'll be the team to beat." She gave Sara a wide smile. "You are both college educated after all."

Sara tried to hide her grin, but her eyes showed her delight.

"Well, yes, we will be a force to be reckoned with. I think we've got a good chance of winning that prize." Robert smiled. "I wouldn't mind taking Sara out for supper."

Sara blushed and gave him a shy smile. She couldn't believe how it had worked out.

Oliver's competitive nature took over. "I'll give you a run for your money, Reverend."

"I?" Ellie said indignantly. "This team has two people remember?"

Oliver scowled and exhaled loudly. "Yeah, so don't slow me down. Princess."

Ellie slammed her hands on her hips and pursed her lips. "Just you don't slow me down, Constable. I attended the finest college in Calgary and graduated with honors. What about you?"

"Book learning isn't everything."

"Well, let's see." She turned to the Reverend. "We've got this Reverend, just you wait and see."

"Do you think so?"

"What if the losing team buys the winning team coffee?" Ellie offered ignoring Oliver's protest.

He rolled his eyes and then nodded. "Alright.

The reverend chuckled. "You're on."

"Okay." Oliver shrugged. "Let's get this over with."

They walked up to the mayor who was holding out envelopes containing their first clue. Oliver put his hand out for it, but Ellie snatched it before he could. He shook his head and shrugged. "Well read it then."

She walked a few steps away from the group and Oliver followed.

Slipping open the envelope she pulled out a piece of paper. Looking around at all the teams huddled together examining the clues, She read aloud,

"To access my contents, you must pull a chain, if you stand beneath me it may feel like rain."

Ellie frowned. "Pull a chain...?"

Oliver took off running and Ellie groaned. "Constable?" She hoisted her skirts and ran after him. "Wait."

Oliver stopped and scowled. "Can't you keep up? I thought you were college-educated."

"I might if I knew where we were going?"

"It's the water tower," he spat as if she should know. "Come on, Princess." He hurried away.

Oliver made it to the water tower behind the town before anyone else. Standing beneath was Christopher Mikkleson. "Cannot give you your clue till your partner arrives. Sorry Constable, 'tis the rules."

Oliver groaned and stepped back to wait as three other teams turned up, collected their clues, and left. Ellie finally arrived, puffing slightly from the exertion. "What took you so long?"

"I couldn't run as fast. I'm a small girl, not a strong man, and it's not so easy in all these layers."

Oliver rolled his eyes. "I knew you'd make me lose."

"We're supposed to be a team, we need to work together, and use both our strengths."

"Fine." He spat. "Get the clue."

She fetched it and hurried over as they watched three teams in the distance carrying firewood. Pulling the card from the envelope she read again.

"To get your next clue, build a campfire and set a kettle to boil. When the kettle sings you'll receive your clue."

"Come on." Oliver gripped her arm. "This'll be easy. I can make a fire."

Ellie grimaced, she sincerely hoped there would be at least one task that relied on her and not just him. She had no idea how to make a fire.

Oliver grabbed up some wood and hurried to a circle set up for the job. Ellie snatched a provided coffeepot. "I'll fill this up."

Oliver nodded. "At least there's something you can do. I'll have this going by the time you get back."

She arrived back from the creek as flames were kissing the wood. She placed the coffeepot on the stand as Oliver stoked up his fire. They turned to look at the teams around them, seven fires were now going and others were arriving. "We might actually win this." Oliver chuckled. "If all the challenges are this easy." He grinned as the coffeepot began to sing.

Mrs. Mikkleson ran over and handed them an envelope.

"Tanner's Bridge." Oliver tried to keep the excitement out of his voice. He had to admit he was enjoying himself, despite his choice of partner. After several hours they were in the lead by a long way. "Think you can keep up or do I have to carry you?"

"I can keep up." Ellie scowled, and nudged the borrowed horse into a canter to follow him.

"Good, because we are in the lead, don't wanna lose because of you."

Ellie sucked in a deep breath, determined not to say something she'd regret.

"Come on." Oliver led the way to the bridge. Finding a clue pinned to a tree, they worked out they needed to catch a fish and bring it to the finish line to claim their prize.

Oliver grinned. "Ever caught a fish, Princess?"

"No." She thrust her arms across her chest.

"Well, you just stand there and watch and try not to get into any trouble. I don't have time to rescue you today."

Ellie scowled as he dug around to find a worm, threaded it on the provided hook and line, and thrust it into the water. Both stood in silence as they waited.

After a time, a tug on his line made Oliver jerk the rod abruptly in the air. "Ahh. Lost him." He groaned and went to pull in the line to rebait it, but it was snagged so he tugged harder. The line snapped and he slipped off the bank and into the water.

Ellie stifled a laugh as he fell with a loud splash. As he sat up, he groaned and gripped his ankle.

Instinctively Ellie splashed into the shallow water, ignoring her skirts getting wet. "Are you alright, Constable?"

Oliver removed a hand from his ankle. "I think I must have sprained it."

She squatted down to examine the ankle and he smirked as he lowered his hand into the water and flicked it up to splash her.

"Huuuh." She gasped and stepped back suddenly, falling into the water onto her bottom. She groaned loudly and looked up at him and scowled. "You're not hurt at all. That's not funny."

"I thought so." He grinned and stood up from the water, holding a hand out to her to help her up.

She scowled at him again. "I don't need your help, thank you." She stood and quickly climbed out of the water, her wet skirts clung to her legs. "Thanks to you, now I'm soaking wet."

"But, I notice you jumped in to save me without a thought. You must care for me more than I thought."

Her eyes blazed with fire. "I'm a nurse, Constable. I told you earlier, it's my job to help people who are hurting, no matter how irritating they are."

Oliver rolled his eyes and walked up to her. "It's just in good fun. A little water never hurt anyone, Princess."

She sneered and folded her arms. "We still have a fish to catch. So get to it, Mr. Funny"

"As you wish, Your Highness." Oliver saluted her sarcastically.

A growl from the trees brought both heads up as a cougar stepped out. Oliver moved his hand to his holster. "Do not move."

Ellie froze to the spot and watched the menacing cat. She'd read about Mountain lions and what they could do to a grown man. They'd never be able to outrun it.

Oliver pulled out his gun slowly and held it out toward the cat. "Back away very slowly." He didn't take his eyes off the cougar. "I'd like to avoid taking his life if I can."

Oliver waited till Ellie was up the bank, then fired a shot just in front of the mountain lion. With a gravelly roar, the cat skipped away.

He sighed with relief and walked out of the water and up the bank. Finding Ellie sitting on a stump shivering. "Mountain lion's gone, I doubt he'll be back."

"Good." She stood up. "Did you get a fish?"

"That doesn't matter. You need to get back so you don't catch your death of cold."

She squinted. "I didn't know you cared."

"I'm not completely without compassion, Princess. If you're cold we need to get you back, can't have the nurse being out of action."

"I wouldn't be so cold if you didn't make me wet." She growled at him.

"I wouldn't have to do that if you weren't such a princess. I was just trying to have some fun and get you involved, up till that point I'd been running the race on my own."

She thrust her hands on her hips and her cheeks grew red as she stormed at him. "On your own? Well, I never." She lifted her wet skirts from around her ankles and marched away. "And don't bother following me." She called over her shoulder.

Oliver shook his head and jogged away in the other direction, taking a shortcut through the forest towards town.

The reverend and Sara met her on the road. Robert carried a fish attached to his line. "Hey, what happened to you?" Both frowned as they approached Ellie.

Ellie gritted her teeth and scowled at them. "Ask the Mountie." She hastened her pace and headed for home.

Reverend Oldfield turned to Sara and both snickered. "I thought they might come to blows."

Sara tucked her lips under. "I feel a bit guilty about that."

"Why would you feel guilty?" What does it have to do with you?"

"I um...." She shrugged and her face reddened.

"Miss Conway, what have you been up to?" he chuckled.

"Well, I uh... I suggested to the Mayor they'd make a good pair..." She held her hands behind her and tried to look nonchalant.

Robert stopped walking and squinted at her. A sly smile crossed his face. "You orchestrated it?"

"Mmmmhmmm." She blushed.

He stroked his beard and raised his brows. "And did you orchestrate this too?" He gestured to her and then to himself.

"Mmmhmmm." She dropped her eyes to examine her shoes.

The pastor nodded and thought for a moment.

Sara's heart raced. It wasn't exactly a heartfelt confession of love but she couldn't go back now.

"Well then, I guess we'd better get back and claim our prize. I'd love to take you out for supper."

Her eyes flashed up to meet his and a look of astonishment crossed her face. "You would?"

"Well, that's the prize, isn't it? A free supper."

Her face fell and she nodded, it was merely him claiming the prize.

"But tomorrow evening, I'm paying."

Sara raised her head again. "I don't understand."

He walked to her and smiled. "I've had such a great time with you today. You're a bright and talented girl and I can't believe you caught a fish before I did." He chuckled, holding up the large catfish.

"I grew up with five brothers. I had no choice but to learn to fish."

"I'm glad. I admit, I was glad the way this turned out. I was hoping we'd win so I'd have an excuse to take you to supper then I hoped to convince you to go out again. But to know you orchestrated this on purpose because you wanted to spend time with me is thrilling. So, let's get back, claim our prize, and have a free supper on the town."

"I'd like that." She bit her lip.

"Come on." He put a hand gently on her back and they hurried toward town.

Nine

Now clean and dry, the Mountie strolled into the café, hoping for some supper. He smiled as he noticed the reverend in the corner dining with Sara. He walked over and smiled. "I hear congratulations are in order."

"Yes." Robert winked at Sara. "Turns out I had the best teammate after all."

"Lucky you." Oliver grimaced.

"We saw Miss Taylor on the road, she was dripping wet. What happened?"

Oliver grimaced again. "I'll tell you some other time. You two enjoy the spoils of your win. I'll leave you to it."

"Thank you, Constable." Robert nodded and then grinned at Sara.

Oliver took a seat at the back corner of the room and nodded to Miss Jayne.

"I'll be right there, Constable." The café was fairly full with people celebrating the fun day out. It'd brought much joy and laughter to the townsfolk and a jovial atmosphere filled the air. Light music played on a victrola in the corner of the room and candles flickered, making the shadows dance on the walls.

Oliver was perusing the menu when Ellie walked in. She didn't notice the Mountie in the corner at first, but she smiled at Sara. She approached and grinned, Sara's eyes were shining as she dined with Reverend Oldfield. "Hello, you two. I hear you won."

"Yes." Sara smiled. "Thanks to the reverend."

Robert shook his head. "I couldn't have done it without you. I think we worked well together as a team."

"Glad someone did," Ellie smirked.

"What happened?" Sara asked. "You two were way ahead of us. We thought you'd beat us all by hours."

"We would've won if someone hadn't thought it funny to try to drown me."

A scoff from the back corner made Ellie's head snap up. She scowled and groaned. "What are you doing here.?

"Having supper, Princess. What does it look like?" He gestured to his food. "You look a little drier than the last time I saw you." He scoffed.

Ellie took a deep breath and marched up to him. "Wipe that smirk off your face, Constable. I am not amused."

"Come on, Miss Taylor. It was just a little water, why are you bent out of shape about it? Is it because you can't handle losing?"

"We lost because of you." She thrust her hands on her hips.

"Really? I'm not the one who walked away."

"I didn't want to spend another minute with you, and I still don't. I'm not hungry." She spun on her heels and marched out.

Oliver sat back in his seat and looked around at all the eyes watching him. He smiled, shrugged, and turned back to his meal. *That's why I don't have any interest in women, they are so hard to understand. I thought she'd appreciate the playful gesture.* He shrugged again and slurped at his coffee as everyone turned back to their meals.

* * * *

"Excuse me, Nurse." Oliver helped a man to hobble into the clinic.

"What is it?" She smiled at the injured man, refusing to make eye contact with the Mountie. He attempted to describe what had happened but she ignored him completely and turned to the injured man instead.

"Hello, I'm Nurse Taylor. What's your name?"

"Charlie Durham, Ma'am." The man wheezed out.

"What is the problem, Mr. Durham?"

"Cut me leg." He coughed loudly.

"Let me see. It seems you have a nasty cough too, Sir."

"It's a miner's cough," Oliver stated.

Ellie scowled at him but nodded. "You're a miner, Mr. Durham?"

"Was, till I 'urt me leg, been givin' me trouble for some time."

"Alright, let's take a look."

Oliver snickered and stood back as the man lifted his legs onto the bed.

Ellie grimaced, she could smell the wound before he could even roll up his trouser legs. "Gangrene." She swallowed back the nausea and reached for her small scissors. "We'll have to get this cleaned up urgently. I hope we won't have to take off your leg."

"Please, Miss, I can't lose my leg. I gots a family to feed, 'tis why I ain't' stopped till now, just 'ad to keep going, but the Constable, says I gotta get help for it."

"If you can handle it. Or I can do the amputation for you. It's not a job for a delicate princess."

Ellie spun around, fire blazed in her eyes. "Why are you still here, Constable? I have this under control."

"I'm just offering my help. Cutting bone can be tough."

"If I want your help, I'll ask for it. Now you are welcome to stay. I can't make you leave, but I will have no more unsolicited advice, thank you."

The Mountie gave her a mock salute and stepped back to watch. *I give her ten minutes before she passes out cold.* He'd seen his fair share of gangrene and knew the only option was to amputate.

She braced herself, slid her scissors up Mr. Durham's trouser leg, and pulled down the stocking hiding the infected wound. It was wrapped tightly in bandages, sticky from the ooze that seeped from the wound.

The bandages were stuck to the wound, so she had to soak them off, at last exposing the stinking rotting flesh. She swallowed and steeled herself. "This is pretty bad, Sir. How long has it been like this?"

"Got the cut about a month ago, been like this two weeks or so." He looked up at her, his eyes appealing to hers. "Will I lose me leg?"

She dabbed at the wound with sterile gauze, causing the man to wince. "Not necessarily."

The Mountie snickered. She silenced him with a scowl and continued. "If it's not too far along, Bromine treatment may be a solution, at least it will stop the infection from getting worse and it may be possible to just excise the damaged flesh."

"Excise?"

"Yes, I'd cut away the flesh that can't be saved and seal up the wound."

"But I'd keep me leg?"

"I hope so. It's not a promise, Sir. I have to investigate this wound and see how bad it really is under all this ooze. Once I get it cleaned up, I'll have more answers for you."

Oliver smirked and quietly left the room. *She's stronger than I thought.* He had to admit he was rather impressed with her manner and her ability. She treated all her patients with kindness and was a clever and capable nurse. "Perhaps I've been a little unfair." He admitted. "Maybe she's not as pampered as I thought." He smiled as he stepped out into the fall sunshine. The reverend and Sara walked around the corner. Robert carried the teacher's books and their eyes sparkled with love for one another. School had just gone back and the students were doing well under her tutelage.

Oliver couldn't help but envy their happiness. The pair had been courting for the three weeks since the scavenger hunt and they were blissfully happy. He nodded to the pair as they approached. "Reverend, Miss Conway."

"Good day, Constable." Sara smiled.

"How's school going?"

"Very well, best start to a year yet." She grinned and looked shyly up at the reverend. "There might be multiple reasons for that."

Robert squeezed her arm, and a wide grin crossed his face. "I think so." He looked back at the Mountie. "Have things improved with Miss Taylor?"

Oliver grimaced. "Sadly, no. She's still very icy toward me. She is speaking to me, but only as a nurse."

"Give her time, Constable," Sara encouraged him. "She'll come round."

"We'll see." The Mountie nodded. "Well, I must get to my...." His face lit up and he grinned. "What on earth." He took off at a run toward the stagecoach platform.

Two women exiting from the stagecoach turned as the man ran towards them. Both faces lit up.

Oliver wrapped the older woman in his arms and kissed her hair. "Ma, what are you doing here?" He released her and reached for his youngest sister. "Gracie. I can't believe you are both here."

"I saved up my wages so we could come to visit, since you missed Maryanne's wedding."

Oliver grinned and hugged both women again, kissing first one, then the other on the cheek. "This is a wonderful surprise. How long can ya stay."

"Only a week, I'm afraid, we gotta get back. I only got a few weeks off work."

"Where can we stay, it's been a long trip and we're exhausted." Grace yawned.

"Come on, I'll take you to the boarding house." He scooped up the two suitcases and led the two women he loved the most in the whole world up the street.

The reverend and Sara stood by watching and caught Oliver's wide grin. He stopped and smiled at the couple. "Reverend, Miss Conway, I'd like to introduce you to my mother and sister. Diana Nelson and Grace Nelson." He turned to the women. "Ma, Gracie, this is Reverend Robert Oldfield and Miss Sara Conway. She's our teacher."

"Lovely to meet you both." Diana nodded.

"You too. I hope you enjoy your stay in Golden Oaks." Robert smiled.

"Thank you, Reverend."

"I'd best get these two to the boarding house." Oliver nodded.

He marched them in the front door and met Mrs. Palmer scrubbing the front windows. "Ma'am." He gestured to his mother and sister. "Got you some boarders." His face beamed, he was so proud to have them come to his town.

"Very good." The woman put down her rag, wiped her hands on her apron, and led them into the foyer. "Follow me and I'll show you where you can stay."

*   *   *   *

Ellie sighed loudly as she climbed the stairs to her room. She was exhausted. "Thank you, Lord, that Mr. Durham will keep his leg." She would allow herself time for supper and a bath, then she'd return to keep a close eye on his wounds. She sighed again as she reached the upstairs landing and walked out into the small sitting room. Two ladies she had never met before were seated drinking tea on the two small setees. "Hello." She gave them a tired smile. She knew she must look rather haggard from a long day but she couldn't be impolite.

"Hello." Both women returned her smile. Ellie walked over to them. "I'm Ellie Taylor. Are you new to town?"

"We're just here for a short visit, a week at most."

"That's wonderful, do you have family in town?"

"Yes." Diana smiled. "My son lives here."

Ellie nodded, the pride on the woman's face was evident.

"This is my daughter, Grace."

"Hi, Grace, lovely to meet you."

"Won't you sit down and join us, Miss Taylor." Grace offered.

"For a short time, I must change before supper, but I have a little time." Ellie sat down. "So, what do you think of our town?"

"It's lovely. We've been a short time but my son has shown us around. He tells me all about the place in his letters."

"Writes faithfully every week," Grace added.

"That's wonderful." Ellie wasn't likely to know who the man was, so she humored the woman and played along. "What has he been telling you?"

"He describes the town and the people."

"Oh, yes." Ellie smiled at Diana.

"We call them 'his adventures.' Sometimes I think he's exaggerating some of the things that happen. They seem so ridiculous." Grace chuckled.

"Yes, we all laugh out loud." Diana smiled.

"Oh. He sounds like quite a character. What kind of things?"

"He described the building of the schoolhouse and said that the pastor slipped off the ladder and hit the ground. The way he described it had us all laughing madly." Grace added.

"And there is that woman he keeps writing about." Diana chuckled. "The wealthy one."

Ellie raised her brows. "Oh, yes. What did he say about her?"

Grace chuckled. "I don't think she's real. He'd never spend that much time with a wealthy woman. He said she's nothing more than a princess."

Ellie tried to keep the horror from her face. "A Princess?"

Grace covered her mouth and giggled. "That's what he calls her, 'of the manor born' he said and very stuck up. Struts around in her finery and feathers like she owns the place."

"Is that right?" Ellie could feel the heat rising. "Anything else?"

"He said she was in some kind of game with him a while back and slipped and fell in the water and he had to rescue her because she was delicate."

"Did he just?" Ellie scowled at Mrs. Nelson. "She sounds interesting."

Grace nodded. "She's got quite a temper apparently. He claims he despises her."

Mrs. Nelson looked up. "Yet he spends more time describing her than anyone else. He's never told me her name or what she's doing on the frontier."

"She's a nurse," Ellie said through gritted teeth. "Now, if you don't mind I need to go and get cleaned up for supper." She worked very hard to keep her cool. "Nice to meet you, Mrs. Nelson, Miss Nelson." She stood and walked away.

Diana and Grace looked at each other and squinted. "How did she know our name was Nelson?"

Mrs. Nelson looked at her daughter. "I'm not sure, perhaps we told her and didn't remember."

Grace shrugged. "I suppose we must've."

Ellie sat in the bathtub and let the hot water soothe her. Her face and heart were nearly as hot as the water that she sat in. She seethed and fought to get her feelings in check. "Who does he think he is?" She shook her head, "Well I'll show him who's a princess."

*   *   *   *

"That was a lovely dinner, thank you, Miss Jayne."

"You're most welcome, Mrs. Nelson. It's lovely to meet you."

"And you, dear. You have a lovely café."

"Thank you. I'm rather proud of it."

"You should be," Grace said. "That was a delicious cake."

Oliver grinned and passed Jayne two one-dollar notes. "Thanks, Miss Jayne. We appreciate it." He turned to his mother and sister as Jayne began clearing the table. "We have time for a stroll by the river before we lose light, what do you think?"

"I'd love that. Work off our supper." Diana smiled.

"Come on then." He gestured to them, helped his mother stand up, and passed both women their shawls. "The river is one of my favorite spots in town. It's so tranquil." He told them as they approached the small brook.

"Look at those beautiful daffodils." Grace grinned, hurrying to the very edge of the river where a large patch of the happy blooms grew. She leaned down to sniff them, and a butterfly flew out of one. She gasped in fright as it fluttered into her face. She stepped back abruptly.

"Look out!" Oliver lunged towards her, too late to prevent her from twisting her ankle and falling back into the river. She struck her head on the river bottom and lay in the water.

"Oh no." Oliver leaped in, scooped her up, and hurried her to town, with his mother running as fast as she could manage behind them.

He burst through the doors of the infirmary. "Miss Taylor," he called. "Miss Taylor?"

"What on earth?" Ellie stood from Mr. Durham's bedside and hurried out into the main room. "Oh, Constable." She swallowed back angry retorts and observed the scene.

Mrs. Nelson hurried through the door, breathing deeply from exertion.

"Ellie." Oliver's voice seemed contrite and desperate. "Please, my sister fell into the river."

Ellie smiled. A patient was a patient regardless of who they were. "Put her down." She gestured to the bed with a clean sheet thrown over the top.

Oliver placed her down gently and stepped back. He linked his arm around his mother and bit his lips together.

Mrs. Nelson eyed her son and frowned. He hadn't mentioned that the woman he'd been writing about was so beautiful or so capable. She was almost certain she knew why he'd covered so many pages about her, but he didn't realize it yet. Now wasn't the time to confront him about it, Gracie needed them.

"How long has she been out?" Ellie asked as she lifted one eyelid and then the other.

"About fifteen to twenty minutes."

Ellie nodded and began unbuttoning the woman's blouse. Oliver turned his head slightly but needn't have worried, after unfastening two buttons Ellie slipped her stethoscope inside, to listen to the woman's heart.

A moan escaped from the girl and both Oliver and his mother gasped, stepping forward. "Gracie? Can you hear me?" Oliver asked.

Ellie shot him daggers and turned back to place her hand on the girl's forehead. "You're okay, Miss Nelson, listen to my voice."

Grace groaned again and her eyes flicked open. "Ohhhhhhh." She groaned even louder. "Where am I?"

"In our infirmary. I'm Nurse Taylor and you've had a nasty bump to the head." Ellie's kindness touched both Mountie and his mother watching on. Mrs. Nelson looked up at Oliver and gave him a knowing nod. He frowned, confusion owning his face. He shrugged and turned back to look at his sister.

"My head hurts."

"Of course it does. Once I can ascertain the extent of your injuries, I'll give you something for the pain."

The younger woman gave her a nod and a wry smile.

Ten

Oliver raced into the infirmary, a look of panic on his face. "What is it? Jimmy Carlson came and got me, said you needed me urgently." He looked at his mother and fell into the seat next to her.

"Yes, Constable. I'm afraid your sister has taken a turn for the worse."

Oliver's face fell and creased up. "What are you saying?"

"I'm saying I believe she has Pneumonia."

"Pnuemonia?"

"She started to fit overnight and has a high fever."

"What does that mean, Nurse?" Mrs. Nelson was much calmer and more pragmatic than her son. "What is her prognosis?"

"She's young and otherwise strong and healthy, she's got every chance of surviving."

Both released their breaths. "That's a relief."

Ellie looked at the Mountie. "But, we must remain vigilant. Someone must remain with her all the time so we can monitor any changes. The sooner we notice them, the sooner they can be treated."

"I'll stay with her," Mrs. Nelson offered.

"You can't twenty-four hours a day, you do need some rest as well or you'll be no good to her."

"I'll relieve Ma when needed." Oliver squeezed his mother's hand. "We'll make sure Gracie isn't alone." He sighed loudly.

"Now, Son." Mrs. Nelson gave Oliver a stern frown. "You aren't to blame yourself."

"But I wanted to go walk by the river. I was showing off my town. If I hadn't she'd be..."

Mrs. Nelson put a finger on his lips. "No blame. Let's just work to get her well."

Oliver leaned in and kissed his mother's forehead. "Of course, Ma. You're right."

"I'll take first watch," The older woman offered.

"Excellent. I'll sleep in the second recovery room next door. Fetch me if you need me. I'll go now and see if Miss Jayne will have some food delivered for you."

"I can do that." Oliver offered, glad to have something to do.

"Thank you." Ellie gave him a curt smile. Feeling bad for him and his situation didn't negate the anger she felt towards him.

He smiled and hurried out of the room. Stopping just outside he drank in the cool September evening air and sighed. "Lord, please save my sister." He leaped off the boardwalk and hurried to the café.

Mrs. Nelson took her place next to her daughter's bedside. Ellie checked on Grace and took her temperature.

"How is she really?" the older woman asked.

Ellie smiled. "She's very sick, Mrs. Nelson. But I will do my very best and give all that I have to see her well."

Mrs. Nelson gripped her hand and looked into her eyes. "I know it was you my son was talking about, and I want you to know I'm sorry for my careless words."

"That's alright, Mrs. Nelson, it's not your words that hurt me..." She blinked back a tear and sniffed.

"He's wrong you know?"

"Wrong?"

"He's wrong about you. You're a wonderful caring woman and I'm confident he'll see it in time. Give him a chance. He's a loving man really."

"What are you saying?" Ellie frowned.

"I know he says he doesn't want to marry but I know in his heart he really does want that."

"Why are you telling me this?"

"Because I think he admires you."

"Me?"

"Yes."

"Hardly, he despises me. He calls me princess and he doesn't mean it kindly." She sneered.

"I'm not so sure."

"He's never shown me anything other than indifference. I'm sorry, ma'am. I know he's your son but he's been awful to me since I first arrived." She blushed. "And I've risen to the occasion, I'll admit."

Mrs. Nelson nodded. "We'll see, dear."

"We'd be horrible together, we can't get through a single conversation without biting each other's heads off."

The woman grinned. "That kind of passion often turns into the strongest kind of love."

"Love? But we hate each other, we'd be terrible together."

"Honestly, dear. I can't think of two people better suited for each other."

"We'd kill each other." Ellie was mortified.

"We'll see." Mrs. Nelson smiled. "We'll see."

Ellie shrugged. "Well, I'll be in the recovery room next door, just call out or come and wake me if you need me."

"Thank you, Nurse, you're most kind."

"It's my pleasure, Mrs. Nelson." Ellie smiled.

Kicking off her shoes, Ellie climbed onto the recovery room bed and pulled a blanket up around her neck, she'd catch a bit of sleep before getting up to check on Grace in the night. She thought about Mrs. Nelson's words. "Oliver and I would kill each other." She reiterated out loud. "Wouldn't we?" she frowned and tried to consider the idea. She grimaced as she thought about just how irritating he was and besides he despised her, didn't he? She shrugged and turned over. Still, it was some time before she could shut her mind off to get to sleep.

*   *   *   *

Ellie stepped out into the main clinic and took a deep breath. She paused and stretched her back then exhaled loudly. "Thank you, Lord." She murmured under her breath. Walking to the counter in the corner of the room she filled a cup with cold water and took it into the recovery room.

Grace lay back with her eyes open, weak but alert. Ellie took the seat next to her and smiled up at Mrs. Nelson then back at the girl. "How are you feeling, Grace?"

"Tired," the girl managed.

"I'm not surprised. Your body has been working hard this last little while. Your fever broke overnight." Ellie passed her the cup and helped her to drink. "Just small sips at this stage."

Grace nodded and lay her head back down. "Now you sleep, you'll be up and about in no time." Ellie patted the girl's shoulder, pulled the bedclothes up around her neck, and stood to leave.

Mrs. Nelson followed her out. "Now what?"

Ellie smiled. "Now we get her strong again so she can travel home."

"I'm most grateful to you, Miss Taylor. You've saved my girl's life..."

Both women's heads turned as the Mountie strode in.

"How is she?" his voice held concern and hope.

"Go and see for yourself." His mother smiled.

Oliver grinned and hurried into the room. "Sis?" He touched her arm, relieved to see the fever was gone.

"Fever broke overnight," Ellie said.

"I'm going to be fine, Ollie," Grace managed.

Oliver grimaced, only his baby sister ever got away with calling him Ollie. He bent down and kissed her forehead. "I'm glad." He smiled then stood and exhaled loudly. Impulsively he turned and lunged to embrace Ellie. "Thank you," he murmured into her hair. Catching himself, he released her as abruptly as he had embraced her, nodded to his mother, and hurried out the door.

Ellie's mouth fell open and she stammered at his retreating figure. "I... umm... you're... you're welcome." She took a deep breath to try to still her heart. There was something about being held in those strong arms that had caught her completely off guard.

Mrs. Nelson eyed the flustered girl and chuckled internally. *They'll see it in time.* She followed her son out, shivering as the icy wind reminded them that the snow would be arriving at any time.

*   *   *   *

"Nurse Taylor."

Ellie looked up as Oliver strode in. "What do you need, Constable?"

"I uh...." He walked further in. "I just put my mother and sister on the stage."

"I see, I trust they got away alright?" Ellie tried to keep her tone even.

Oliver frowned at her. *Is she still angry about the scavenger hunt? I guess now that Grace is well she can drop the act.* "Yes, they did."

"Good."

Both stood in silence for a time.

"Did you just come to tell me that?" Ellie thrust a hand on her hip. "I have patients to see."

"No. I came to thank you." His voice was sincere, there was a note of contrition to his tone.

Ellie raised her brows. "You already did."

He stepped closer. "Not properly. I want to apologize and say I've misjudged you, somewhat."

She eyed him but did not speak.

"You're a good nurse, you saved my sister's life."

"It's my job, Constable."

"I know, but I want you to know... I'm grateful."

Ellie tilted her head. "That must have hurt you to admit." She scowled.

Oliver shook his head. "I'm trying to apologize to you. Are you so stuck up you can't even accept my words?"

"I didn't hear an apology."

"I'm sorry." His voice was genuine.

Ellie thrust her hands on her hips. "For what exactly?"

"Well, for the things I've said..."

"Which things? If you're going to apologize then apologize."

Oliver shook his head and squinted at her. "You're impossible you know that? I didn't have to come here just now."

"Then why did you come?"

"I told you, to apologize."

"And yet no apology has come."

"I said I'm sorry." His frustration was growing.

"Sorry, for what? Splashing me, calling me a princess, the lies you've told about me?"

"Lies?" Oliver was mortified. "I've told no lies."

Ellie raised her brows. "Not even in letters to your mother?"

Oliver sucked his lips under and lowered his eyes. He looked up. "I may have exaggerated for comic benefit..."

"Comic benefit? So, what? Now I'm a laughing stock to provide entertainment for your family?" She thrust both hands on her hips. "You despise me so much you use me as fodder for your letters home?"

Oliver cringed and gave her a sad smile. "That's not what I meant. I don't despise you. Truth is I admire your dedication to your patients and I am genuinely sorry."

"Your mother told me the things you said about me. She didn't know who she was speaking to but you made it quite clear what you think of me. Nothing but a stuck-up pampered princess." She seethed. "I'm not interested in some sniveling apology that makes you feel better because I helped your sister." She fixed her eyes on his and scowled. "I didn't do it for you."

Oliver held her gaze for a time and nodded. "For whatever reason, I'm grateful." He nodded again, spun around, and marched out.

Ellie stood staring at the door for a time then exhaled loudly and walked out of the clinic, shut the door, and hurried to the boarding house. She raced up the stairs, threw herself on her bed, lifted her knees, buried her head in her arms, and cried. Finally regaining control of her emotions she sat up. "Why does what he thinks of me bother me so much? Why can't I let go of my anger?" Ever since he had embraced her, she'd not been able to get him out of her mind. Seeing him just now made her want to throw herself in his arms, but she was much too hurt and angry and more than a little confused. "What is happening, Lord? I've never disliked a man more than him, and yet I can't stop wishing I would see him again. Then when I do see him all I can think about is the things he's written home to his mother about me." She wiped at her eyes and grimaced. "Oh, he really is the most infuriating man."

Eleven

"More coffee, Constable?" Miss Jayne lifted the coffee pot to him.

"Certainly. You make excellent coffee."

"Thank you. Your roast meal will be out shortly."

"No hurry, Miss Jayne." He smiled as the woman nodded and headed through the double doors and out into the kitchen.

"Mind if I join you?"

Oliver looked up at the reverend and gestured to the chair opposite him. "Good evening, Reverend. Not out with your girlie tonight?"

Robert grinned. "No, she wanted to spend some time planning out the Christmas pageant. She's getting an early start so she can have four to five weeks to get it right."

"She did a fine job last year."

Robert nodded as Miss Jayne strode back out with the coffee pot and poured him a cup. "Yeah, she didn't have as many distractions last year."

Oliver sipped at his coffee and scoffed. "You look rather pleased with yourself."

"Can you blame me? I found a wonderful woman."

"Do I hear wedding bells?"

Robert grinned. "In time. For now, I'm just content to love her. There is nothing better than to be loved by a woman."

"Wouldn't know." Oliver shrugged and curled his mouth up.

"I thought you told me you'd been engaged once?"

"Yeah, but she never loved me. I know that now. If she did she wouldn't be married to some other man." He grimaced. "Woman do nothing but hurt ya. Can't even apologize to them without having your intentions questioned."

Robert placed his cup down and tilted his head to the side, his face asking the question.

Oliver sighed and sipped at his coffee again. "I went to apologize to Ellie, to thank her for saving my sister's life and I got an earful."

"Oh. I'm sorry." Both men sat drinking their coffee in silence for a time. Then Robert squinted. "I didn't think she meant anything to you."

Oliver shrugged. "She doesn't."

"Then why does that bother you so much."

"It doesn't. I'm just making conversation."

Robert sat back and scratched his chin. "Mmmhmmm." He took another sip of his coffee and squinted at Oliver. "You should tell her how you feel."

"What are you saying? I tried to apologize, and I got nowhere." Another grimace followed by a loud sigh.

"Have you tried telling her the truth?"

"Truth?"

Robert shook his head. "It's as plain as the nose on your face that you love her."

"Don't be ridiculous. I told you I don't ever plan to marry."

"You didn't deny it."

"Yes I did, it's not true."

"If your apology is as good as your denial then I'm not surprised she didn't take you seriously."

"What are you saying, Reverend? What makes you think I'm in love with her?"

"You can't stop talking about her and when you do your eyes light up. Every time I've seen you since your sister got sick you've told me all about Ellie and what she's done for Grace. I don't think you mentioned your sister at all, just the nurse. Your mother told me you write about her non-stop – you know she thinks you're in love with Ellie as well."

"Well, if you could all just stop telling me who I love." Oliver pushed his plate away. "Don't you think that should be up to me?"

"No."

Oliver frowned. "Then who should it be up to, don't I get a say in this?"

"God's in control, you can deny all you like but with the great matchmaker on the case it's only a matter of time."

"I couldn't be in love with her, she barely even speaks to me. She is the stubbornest woman I've ever known and she won't even hear me out."

"Pray, Constable. God will show you."

"I think you're dreaming, Reverend. I'm not interested in having a family and I'm certainly not interested in a pampered princess like her. Yes, she's a good nurse, but what about when the going gets tough, she'll crumble to pieces and I'll have to rescue her all the time. I've got no time for delicate cases. Besides, she won't even speak to me. Now if you'll kindly leave it alone, we can get on with having coffee."

"Alright." Robert drained his coffee and stood up, turning to leave. He took one step then turned back. "But I think you're making a huge mistake. The two of you are perfect for one another and you could be very happy together if you're willing to eat humble pie and go to her with a contrite heart." He hurried out of the café.

Oliver leaned back in his chair for a time, exhaled loudly, and gripped the table with both hands. *She is the most infuriating woman I've ever met. How can the reverend ever think I'd be in love with the likes of her? If I was going to be with a woman it certainly wouldn't be her.*

He looked up as the door opened and grimaced. It was Ellie on the arm of Kevin Johnson, a rather gangly-looking man, new to town. She looked up at him and gave him a smirk, turning to smile at Kevin as he led her to the table next to him. Kevin nodded. "Good evening, Constable."

"Kevin." Oliver forced a smile, stood, pulled some coins from his pocket, and placed them on the table. "If you'll excuse me, I have reports to write." His eyes fell on Ellies, he gave her a barely perceptible frown and hurried out the door, marching as quickly as he could to his office, refusing to make eye contact with anyone he passed.

He closed the door louder than he meant to and tossed his hat on the seat by his desk. Storming into his small quarters he slumped down into the settee before his fire and scowled and let his bitter thoughts run away with him as he tossed the reverend's words back and forth in his mind. "What does she see in Kevin Johnson? I've seen him frequent the saloon and even visit with some of the women that work there." He grimaced, wishing he could abolish the saloon and all its activity. That lifestyle destroyed many good men. "If he gets his claws into her..." The reverend's words circled back around "Why does it bother me so much? I'm not in love with her. I don't even really care about her much..." his words petered out. "Do I?" He stroked his clean-shaven chin. "I can't possibly. I don't even like her."

* * * *

"What's his problem?" Kevin looked up at Ellie.

"He's a bitter man." Ellie scowled. "I don't want to talk about him."

"Was he your beau?"

"No!" Ellie was indignant. "He's the last man on earth I'd care for. He's so arrogant and full of his own importance."

"I see." The man grinned. "I thought he'd jilted ya or something, seems to be an iciness 'tween ya."

"I'd rather not talk about him if you don't mind. Tell me about yourself." She tried to take an interest in him. Kevin was a handsome man she'd seen around town a few times. He'd asked her to supper three times and she'd finally agreed, to get him off her back but he seemed awfully dull, but she wouldn't judge him until she got to know him better. Everyone deserved the benefit of the doubt.

Oliver watched out the window as Kevin led Ellie past the NWMP station on the wide boardwalk towards the boarding house. There was something about him that looked familiar and gave him a bad feeling. He watched as they paused just outside and Oliver could hear their conversation, even though he knew he shouldn't be listening, he pinned his ear to the boards and peered out the gap in the curtains.

"I had a nice evening with you, Miss Taylor."

"Me too. Thank you, Kevin."

"You're most welcome. I'd like to take you out again sometime."

"I suppose that would be alright. What did you have in mind?"

"A beautiful girl like you, city-bred, wouldn't want to be with a countryman like me." He played coy.

Oliver scowled. *He's laying it on pretty thick.*

"I wouldn't mind." Ellie smiled politely. She couldn't work out if Kevin was sincere or not. Until she had a reason not to, she'd enjoy his company. He hadn't turned out to be as dull as she'd first thought. Sure he wasn't like the men back home, and she didn't feel any sparks fly, but he seemed to be a decent and kind man, and she had no reason not to trust him.

"Really?" Kevin smiled. "That's wonderful news. I was wondering if you'd accompany me to the winter dance."

"I've not heard of a dance coming up?" She squinted.

"Mmmhmmm, this Saturday ev'nin' we has one every winter, bout a month 'fore Christmas, just to bring up everyone's spirits before we really get shut in for the winter months."

"That sounds lovely."

"It's not like your city dances."

"Still, it sounds like fun."

"Would you go with me? I sure could like having a pretty girl like you on my arm. Other chaps'd be right jealous."

"I don't see why not, Mr. Johnson. That sounds like fun."

He leaned in and brushed her cheek. "I look forward to it." He grinned and Oliver could see the smirk on his face, but the man turned and guided Ellie up the boardwalk. Oliver could just make out him farewelling her at the boarding house door. She disappeared inside and the man chuckled, smirked again, and strode down the boardwalk. Oliver opened the curtain a fraction wider to watch the man as he disappeared into the saloon. Before the heavy door even swung closed, Oliver observed a saloon girl drape her arms over his neck and the man wrap his arm around hers.

"I have to warn her," Oliver vowed. He considered marching across the road and dragging Kevin out of the saloon, but it wouldn't do any good, what he was doing wasn't illegal and the town had overruled him when he'd tried to suggest closing the saloon. That man was utterly reprehensible.

Oliver got very little sleep that night as he seethed and established a plan to warn Ellie off him.

Twelve

"Constable, here's your mail." Mr. Fraser held out two envelopes.

"Thank you." Oliver lifted both and perused them. A frown crossed his face. "Much obliged, Fraser." He stepped outside, ignoring the icy wind in his face, and stepped into his office. He opened his drawer and slipped one envelope inside, he'd read his mother's letter later. It was the one from HQ that interested him the most.

"Just as I thought." He grimaced. "I knew I'd seen him somewhere." He shoved the letter back inside the envelope, shoved it in his pocket, and marched across to the infirmary. He knocked on the open door. "Excuse me, Miss Taylor. Might I have a word?"

Ellie looked up from updating Mrs. Clarence's file and raised her brows. "What is it, Constable? Come to not apologize again."

"No, this is an entirely different manner. One of some concern to me."

"Regarding?" She stood and walked around the desk to face him.

"Kevin Johnson."

Ellie's face scrunched up and she squinted. "What about him?"

"You're courting right?"

"I wouldn't say that."

"Well, you have an understanding."

"We have no such thing, not that it's any of your business. We had supper together last night, that's all."

"But you are going to the dance with him?"

Ellie squinted. "How do you know that?"

"I overheard you outside the boarding house last night."

"You were eavesdropping? That's low, even for you."

"What's that supposed to mean."

"I knew you were spineless, Constable, but that's further than I thought you'd stoop."

"I didn't mean to, my quarters are right next door. In fact, they cut off a few rooms from the boarding house to build my quarters and the walls are thin."

"But you could've chosen not to listen if you wanted to."

"I was worried about you."

"So that justifies you listening in on a PRIVATE conversation."

"I'm the law, Ellie. If I have concerns I'll take whatever legal measures are needed to keep my people safe."

"Your people? I am not one of your people. I don't need your help or your unsolicited advice."

Oliver exhaled, this was not going as he expected. What had he thought? She'd just be grateful to him and throw herself into his arms? He shook his head and smiled. "Let me try this again. Everyone in this town is my responsibility. I consider all citizens 'my people' because I care about them all. Even you. The safety of the residents of this town is my first priority and if I deem someone is in an unsafe situation I will act."

"And I'm in an unsafe situation am I?"

"Potentially."

Ellie thrust her hands on her hips and leaned in she observed his face and smirked. "Are you jealous, Constable?"

"Jealous?"

"You've obviously come to warn me off Kevin with some kind of evidence of how he's 'unsuitable' and 'you care about my safety.' It sounds like you're jealous."

"What would I be jealous of exactly?"

"Perhaps you wish I was going to the dance with you, spending time with you."

A slow smile crossed his face. "You really are that conceited and full of your own importance, aren't you? Yes, I just spend my days walking around and pining for you. Ellie, it's my job to be suspicious, so I can assure you, this is duty, not jealousy." He hoped that sounded convincing to her, because internally he wasn't entirely sure.

"Okay, I'll bite. What is this oh-so-unsafe situation I find myself in."

Oliver nodded. "Johnson isn't who you think he is."

"Oh, and just who is he?"

"For starters, after he left you he went straight to the saloon."

"Telling tales, Constable. That seems beneath your station." She hoped she kept the shock off her face. "You're grandstanding now. I'm still not convinced you're not just jealous of him because he's twice the man you are." Her conscience pricked her, she couldn't think why she said that, but her heckles were up. "Whatever game you're playing, I don't want any part of it. I am quite able to determine who I can spend time with."

"But you don't know anything about him."

"I don't know anything about you, yet you seem to be 'safe' to be around. Or should I run from you too? Heaven knows I might get some peace and quiet then."

"I'm a Mountie."

"So? That makes you perfect does it?"

"Of course not, but they're very particular about who they let become officers of the law."

"I'll keep that in mind. Now unless there's anything more interesting than you wanting to meddle in my personal life, I'll ask you to leave."

"Miss Taylor, please hear me out."

A woman appearing in the doorway drew her attention. "Mrs. Allerton, come on in." She turned to the Mountie. "You can see I have a patient, so please see yourself out."

"But.... I need to..."

Ellie ignored him and led the older woman over to the bed in the corner. She pulled the curtain around her leaving the Mountie standing alone. He groaned audibly and marched out the door.

He kicked a stone off the boardwalk and slammed the door as he entered his office. Taking out the letter he perused it again. "All I can do is get him to admit it. And it has to be in front of Ellie so she'll see him for who he is." He smirked. "Jealous! Hardly. I'm not sure what he sees in her in the first place. Mind you a wealthy woman would be a good cash cow for a man like him."

*   *   *   *

Oliver arrived at the saloon early, he wasn't thrilled that it was the venue for town functions like this one, but it was the biggest building in town by far and he'd be there to make sure things didn't get out of hand and to keep the families safe. No alcohol or entertainment was permitted on town social nights, instead, the town band played and Miss Jayne and the saloon manager, Mr. Edwin Watts, provided food.

"Ed." Oliver greeted the man.

"Constable." The bartender nodded. "You're early, dance doesn't start for another hour." He gestured to the band setting up in the corner and his workers moving tables and chairs back against the wall to prepare the 'dance floor.'

"Wanna be here early to keep an eye on things."

"You gonna dance this year?"

"I don't think so. I'm on duty."

"Ain't you allowed any fun?" James Cooper asked as he placed a chair on top of one of the round tables.

"I can join in, but it's better I don't. I need to be alert."

"Who are you keeping an eye on?" The saloon owner was an astute man.

Oliver approached the bar, speaking in a low voice he asked, "What do you know about Kevin Johnson?"

Bartender shrugged. "Not much, only been in town a few months. Why do you want to know?"

"No reason in particular, just don't know much about him and I have my reasons to think he's not who he seems."

"Oh, he ain't Kevin Johnson that's for sure."

"Why do you say that?"

"He introduced himself to a chap recently as Edgar then quickly changed to Kevin, like he forgot he was supposed to keep up the ruse. He thought no one noticed but I overheard him."

"Why didn't you say anything to me?"

"Lotsa reasons men change their names, probably running away from a meddling woman." The bartender chuckled. "Ain't my business, long as he keeps spending money 'ere."

Oliver grinned as something occurred to him. "When was the last time he was in here spending money?"

"S'afternoon 'fore we closed to set up for the dance."

"Did he use cash money?"

"What other kind of money is there?" The bartender squinted.

"Sometimes people barter."

The man nodded. "Yes, he paid in cash money."

"Notes or coins?"

The bartender grinned and opened the cash register. He lifted out the drawer and pulled out a note. "Paid me this crisp clean ten-dollar bill. I don't get many of 'ese so I put under 'ere.'" He gestured to the money tray.

"May I see that?"

"What for?"

"I have my reasons."

"You gonna give it back?"

"Maybe. Depends if it helps with my case or not."

"You want me to give you my profits?"

Oliver nodded and grimaced. He reached into his pocket and pulled out a roll of notes. "Here." He passed him two five-dollar bills. "This'll cover it."

The older man scrunched up his face and meant to protest. "Can I 'ave it back if it doesn't help with your case."

"I promise." Oliver held the two notes out to him.

"Alright." The bartender passed over the ten-dollar bill and snatched the two fives from the Mountie's hand as though he might change his mind.

"Thank you." Oliver perused the note carefully, then folded it up and put it in his pocket. "I've gotta run a few errands but I'll be back before the band strikes their first chord."

The bartender merely nodded and the Mountie strode out. Hurrying to his office he unlocked his file cabinet and rummaged through until he found a file he needed. Lifting it out he shut the drawer forcefully then slumped into his chair and opened the file. Flicking through the pages, he paused and lifted a sheet of paper. He lifted the ten-dollar bill and placed it below the drawing, flicking his eyes back and forth to compare the two.

He flipped the note over and examined the other side. "Counterfeit." He grinned. "I've got him." He opened his drawer and pulled out the hand-drawn picture on the wanted poster from HQ. He'd seen that face many times staring down at him from the wall of Canada's most wanted criminals. "Edgar Elliot Fredrickson of Maple Crest, Manitoba. How'd you end up on the prairies?" He spoke to the image. "I guess you thought you could hide here, and we'd never notice. Well, I've got you now and you won't get anywhere near Miss Taylor if I have anything to do with it." A wry smirk of satisfaction crossed the Mountie's face.

He folded the relevant pages and put them in his pocket, filed the brown folder back in the cabinet, and left the office, carefully locking the door behind him. Strolling across to the telegraph office he hurried to send the required alerts, praying backup would arrive quickly. Morris Eagle was the nearest man, stationed at Fort Tender, slightly north and west of his location. By his calculations Eagle could get to Golden Oaks in an hour, provided he left right away.

Thirteen

Oliver was later than he planned to be and by the time he stepped back into the saloon the band had been playing for some time and the room was filled with people dancing. A quick survey of the room told him Ellie was not yet there and neither was Johnson.

He walked the perimeter greeting people and gladly accepted a cup of coffee from Miss Jayne. He leaned against the wall and watched the dancers for a time, smiling at the Reverend holding his sweetheart close while they danced. "He's got it bad." He chuckled at the blissful smile on the man's face.

His head flicked up when the door opened. Ellie and Kevin walked in and Oliver felt himself recoil, unable to take his eyes from her. Her face was radiant and she wore a twisted jewelled band across her forehead like a simple crown. He smiled, "Princess" he whispered as he lowered his eyes to take in the sparkly gown with beads that appeared to dance in the lamplight. He shook his head and frowned as his eyes turned to Johnson. He took her heavy shawl and hung it over chairs at the front of the room where a row of shawls and coats hung.

Oliver dragged his thoughts from Ellie to the job at hand. The telegram he'd received said Morris Eagle was on his way, and he'd not do anything until the Sergeant arrived. In the meantime, he'd keep watch and see to it that man didn't hurt Ellie. He'd make sure she was safe, whether she wanted him to or not.

The man led Ellie toward the beverage stand and the Mountie nodded to both as they passed him. "Good evening, Constable." Ellie flashed him a wide, smug smile.

The flip to his heart caught Oliver off guard. *Perhaps I am jealous, she's so beautiful.* He scolded himself internally. *It doesn't matter, there is no place in your life for a woman, especially not one like Ellie Taylor.*

"Miss Taylor." He nodded.

"I'll get your drink, and meet you back here." Johnson was being extremely gentlemanly.

"Thank you." Ellie grinned at him and flicked her eyes to the Constable's as the other man strode away.

Oliver followed him with his eyes and a deep frown.

"You needn't worry, Constable, he's a gentleman."

"He isn't who you think he is." Oliver frowned and flicked his eyes back to watch the man. He squinted as he watched Johnson pull a roll of bills from his pocket and pass one dollar over to the woman serving drinks. She nodded and fished around in her money box for change. She handed it to him, and he gathered the two drinks and headed back towards them.

Ellie gladly accepted the drink and smiled. "Thank you."

The man nodded and eyed the Mountie. "Constable." He was so confident of his anonymity that he didn't even try to hide.

"Johnson." Oliver folded his arms and clenched his gloved hands against his chest. "Enjoy your evening."

He tried to keep his voice light, while keeping one eye on the door, praying for Eagle's imminent arrival.

Johnson gave her a toothy grin. "You wanna dance?"

Ellie placed her empty glass down and smirked at the Mountie. "I would love to Mr. Johnson."

Oliver gritted his teeth and cast another pensive look towards the door.

It was another half hour before a sergeant strode in. Many heads turned and the music stopped as Oliver marched up to him and saluted. When both Mounties stepped outside the dance resumed, ignoring whatever was happening.

Ellie noticed Johnson flinch as he watched the two Mounties talk. "What is it?"

He frowned, then gave her a relieved smile as the Mounties left the room. "Nothing, just not used to seeing two red coats in this town."

"I'm sure it's nothing." Ellie felt a foreboding feeling wash over her, she ignored it and smiled. "Just Mountie business, nothing to concern us."

"I'm sure you're right." Johnson resumed dancing but did not take his eyes from the door. His body was tense and he gripped Ellie tighter.

Ellie frowned. "Please loosen your grip, you're hurt..." Her voice was cut off by both Mounties walking in, pistols in hand.

Johnson reacted quickly, snatched Ellie into his arms, and pulled his knife from his sheath holding it in front of her neck. "Don't come any closer." His voice was menacing.

"Kevin? What's going on?" Ellie tried to pull away from him. She seethed, not just at this vile man but at the fact the Mountie was right.

"I ain't letting them take me alive."

Screams and terrified gasps filled the room. Men stepped in front of the women and pulled them to the sides of the room away from the knife-wielding man.

Oliver looked around and lifted his hand. "It's alright everyone, we are just here to make an arrest."

Johnson scowled. "Don't come no closer." He poked the point of the knife into Ellie's neck. She flashed frightened eyes at Oliver and stretched her neck as far away as she could.

"Let the lady go, Fredrickson. It's over for you now." Oliver threatened.

"You ain't got no evidence agin me."

"Then why are you holding a woman hostage?" The sergeant asked.

"Because I'm a wanted man, red coats been framing me for years."

"Framing you?" Oliver asked.

"I'm innocent."

"Of what?" The sergeant needed the man's confession.

"They say I been using forged bills. I ain't never seen a forged bill in my life, couldn't even tell ya what they look like."

"That sounds like a confession," Oliver said to the Sergeant.

"You might be right."

"Never." The man gripped Ellie tighter. "I'll kill her if you don't back off. I swear it."

"Let her go, Fredrickson. You've been caught red-handed." He pulled the ten-dollar note from his pocket. "Bartender gave me this – you used it this afternoon."

"I've been set up, it wasn't me. I never seen those notes before."

"Notes? There are more?" The sergeant played dumb.

"I've got one here." Oliver sidled over to the beverage stand and fetched the dollar note. "I'll bet if we check his pockets there are more." He fixed his eyes on Ellie. "He's greedy, money-hungry, and willing to cheat and swindle to get what he wants. According to his file, he finds wealthy women in every town he goes to and exploits money from them." He raised his brows.

Ellie scowled and closed her eyes, she didn't want to know Oliver had been right. Anger brewed in her and she growled then lifted one foot and rammed her back into Johnson's kneecap. Johnson gasped, dropping the knife as he staggered back and grabbed at his knee, groaning loudly.

Oliver reached for Ellie but she pushed past him and stormed out of the saloon. Ignoring the Mounties waiting with a prison wagon she crossed the snow-covered road and headed for her room in the boarding house. She wasn't going to give Oliver the satisfaction of being right.

The younger Mountie watched her go but turned to quickly subdue the man.

Johnson spat on him. "You'll never keep me in prison. I escaped once and I'll do it again."

"Not this time, Fredrickson." The sergeant pulled his handkerchief from his pocket and wiped the saliva from his coat. "You're coming to the fort with me." He forced the man out the door.

Oliver followed, calling over his shoulder. "Carry on."

The room erupted in applause and the dance resumed.

Four constables stood outside waiting. One stepped forward and opened the door to the prison wagon. The Sergeant shoved the man in it and locked the door. Giving one young constable the key he nodded. "Watch him, he's tricky." The four men mounted the wagon front and back.

The Sergeant stepped up onto the front of the wagon and gripped the reins. He saluted Oliver and nodded. "Well done, Constable. Quick thinking."

"Thank you, Sir. Just doing my job."

The sergeant nodded. "I hope you get the girl."

Oliver squinted. "No, Sir, there's no room in my life for a woman or a family."

"I'm married, Nelson. Best choice I ever made. I'm a better man and a better Mountie because of my Annabelle."

Oliver merely nodded. "I understand, Sir."

The sergeant clucked to the horses and hurried away, hoping to make it back to the fort before the snow came.

* * * *

Ellie clung to her pillow and wept. "How can I be so foolish." She sobbed. "I was so determined for Oliver to be wrong..." A knock on the door jarred her from her dark thoughts. "Who is it?" she called as she wiped her eyes.

"Oliver."

Ellie grimaced. "What do you want?" She couldn't explain the mixed emotions that washed through her. She wanted to see him desperately and throw herself in his arms to thank him a hundred times, but at the same time, she wanted to rage and scream and lash out at him.

"Please, Ellie, will you just open the door?" His voice was kind.

She took her time walking to the door, wiping at her cheeks as she walked. She opened it a crack. "What do you want?"

"Please, open the door."

Ellie opened it and glared at him. "What do you want? I suppose you came to say I told you so?" She dropped her head, and her lip trembled.

"No, I came to make sure you're alright." He stepped forward, reached out a hand, and lifted her chin. "And to say I'm truly sorry."

Ellie could only nod and she sniffed back the tears that threatened to overwhelm her again. "I should've listened to you."

Oliver shook his head. "I practically pushed you into his arms. I know that."

"I didn't believe you and I'm sorry."

"Don't be. I'm just glad he didn't hurt you." Ellie blinked at tears and Oliver dared to reach out and draw her into an embrace. "I'm truly sorry," he whispered into her hair.

She nodded and stepped back from him. "Thank you." She wasn't completely ready to forgive him, but she appreciated the compassion in his voice.

"Are you alright?"

"Yes."

Oliver eyed her as if making sure she was certain. "I'll be in my office if you need me, anything at all."

She nodded again.

He leaned forward and brushed her cheek with his knuckles. "I'm glad you're alright, Princess." He winked, turned on his heels, and marched out.

Ellie closed the door and leaned up against it. She closed her eyes and sighed. *Why do I like to be held by him? Nothing's changed, he's still so infuriating.*

Fourteen

"Nurse, Nurse, you gotta help my boy." A frantic voice brought Ellie to the door in a hurry.

"Mrs. Thomas?" She glanced at the boy and grimaced. The telltale red spots on his face brought urgency to her voice "Quick bring him in and lay him on the bed." She gestured to the bed by the wall. "How long has he been like this?" Ellie closed the clinic door.

"Since yesterday." The woman stepped back from her son and frowned as Ellie washed her hands. "Spots came up, yesterday." She hurried to the boy's bedside and examined him. "What is it, nurse?"

"Smallpox." Ellie frowned. "I heard there was an outbreak in Peace River."

"Austin collected a plow from Peace River last week?"

"Has Peter been to school this week?"

"Yes, ma'am. He felt a little hot but he was okay so I sent him to school."

Ellie stifled a grimace. "We're gonna have to quarantine him, Ma'am. This condition is very contagious."

"What does that mean?"

"It means the two of you will have to stay here and not go out anywhere. I've been immunized but most of this town has not." She administered some pain relief for the little boy and carefully showed his mother how to clean the pus-filled lumps that sat on his skin.

"Mrs. Thomas, I have to get some help. This could infect the whole town. We have to act quickly."

"What shall we do?"

"Stay here and continue to soak his skin like I showed you. All we can do for him is keep him comfortable."

"Will he live?"

Ellie gave her a supportive smile. "I hope so," was all she could manage. "But we need to get to the rest of the town and prevent the spread as much as we can. I promise I won't be gone long. I have to get the constable." She sighed. "And hope he'll listen to me."

The mother nodded and took the wet cloth from the nurse. Ellie scrubbed her hand and face the best she could, threw her apron in the trashcan, and snatched the box of vaccinations from the shelf. "Don't let anyone in, alright. Please, it could be dangerous."

Mrs. Thomas managed a brave smile and she nodded. Ellie closed the door behind her and ran up the boardwalk. Sara passed her and smiled. "Ellie?"

Ellie paused. "I can't stop, it's urgent. I'll talk later." Sara frowned but nodded.

"Please be in your office." She flew into the NWMP office and scowled, Oliver wasn't there. "Normally I can't get rid of you and now I need you and you're out."

"What are you doing here?" Oliver stepped into his office. "Didn't you have enough of me the first time? Here for another bite?"

Ellie scowled. "I haven't got time for your games right now, this is urgent, or I wouldn't have come to you."

Oliver's face softened. "Urgent?"

"Mrs. Thomas just brought Peter in, he's got smallpox."

Oliver grimaced. "Ohhhhh. Are we on the brink of an epidemic?"

"Potentially, or I wouldn't be here. Trust me, coming to you for help is not exactly my dream." She looked up abruptly as he gripped her arm, her face curling into a scowl.

"Ellie, tell me what is it you need me to do?"

"Why are you asking me? Aren't you in charge of this town?" Ellie couldn't believe her own words, at a time when the town needed her.

"Ellie, it's Christmas in a few weeks, and this town is on the brink of an outbreak. Do you think we can put aside our animosity for a time and call a truce?"

"A Christmas Truce?"

"Yes, for the sake of the town."

Ellie nodded. "Of course, for now. But don't make the mistake of thinking all is forgotten and forgiven."

"I wouldn't dream of it, Princess." He frowned. *Just when I thought things were getting better between us. Clearly, I have more damage control to do.*

She nodded. "Truce." She put her hand out to shake his.

"Truce." He shook hers and smiled. Taking his hand back he asked again. "What do you advise? I'll follow your lead. I'm the law here but you're the medicine remember, you told me that?"

She smiled and nodded. "We need to vaccinate all the children, they've been in school with Peter all week, and then get word to all the town to stay home, look out for the symptoms and if they see them they are not to leave their homes. I'll come to them with medicine, it'll be a natural quarantine. We can't get everyone to town in this snow, especially with more on the way."

"What's the fatality rate for this?"

Ellie frowned. "Hard to say. It can kill about half the people who are infected, it's worse for children and deadly for unborn babies."

Oliver looked up as his mind processed. "We have, I believe, five expectant mothers in the township, and about thirty-five children."

"I don't have enough vaccines, and I'll need a whole lot more medicine."

"Tell me what you need, and I'll get an emergency shipment in. Anything else?"

"We have to quarantine the town urgently. Please, Oliver, it's essential this doesn't spread any more than it already has. Everyone must stay in their homes. I'll need help to treat everyone, get the reverend on standby, there will be deaths." She grimaced, she'd never called him Oliver before.

Oliver gripped her arm. "We'll come through it."

"Won't be much of a Christmas I'm afraid."

"These are resilient people, they'll get through it. So make a list and I'll call a town council meeting, and we'll get the news out. Where do you want to do the vaccinations?"

"The only safe way will be to go home to home." She grimaced again. "Let's hope the snow doesn't get too thick, it'll make it a lot harder."

"It will however keep everyone indoors. Maybe we should pray for a blizzard, natural quarantine."

"But that makes it harder for me to treat them." Ellie frowned.

"You're right." Oliver nodded.

"I'll need ten to twelve people, vaccinated, willing to help, it's gonna take many hands."

"You've got mine." He raised a hand to brush her cheek. "Sure am glad we have you in this town."

She gave him a reluctant smile and felt her heart flutter as he touched her, but now wasn't time to deal with that emotion, they had an epidemic to prevent. She frowned. "I don't know that this meets the conditions of a truce, Constable. Now we have no time to lose."

Oliver snatched a piece of paper and a pencil from his desk and recorded everything Ellie dictated to him.

"Go get word to as many people as you can. I'll send some telegrams and get what you need on the way."

"I don't want to panic the people. I'm not good at diplomacy."

"Ellie, if it's as urgent as you say, better a little panic than mass deaths later. Get the teacher and reverend, both attended college and I imagine will both be vaccinated. Go door to door. Record any that are sick and then we can regroup."

Ellie nodded, suddenly feeling extremely overwhelmed by the enormity of what lay ahead of her, she threw herself in his arms. "I'm so scared."

Oliver lay his chin on her head. "I am too."

She stepped back to look into his eyes. "You are?"

"I'm always afraid when something seems too big for me, but remember God is bigger than all of this and you can do this. Just promise me you won't risk your own life. The weather is set to be iffy the next week or so."

"But the people need me."

"You're no good to the town if you get sick." His eyes searched hers, suddenly acutely aware of how he would miss her should anything happen.

"They need you too, Constable. Have you been vaccinated?"

"No."

Ellie snatched open the box and pulled out a syringe. "Roll up your sleeve."

"What?"

"Roll up your sleeve."

"You're gonna vaccinate me now?"

"You're no good to me if you catch the pox, Constable. Trust me, this is necessity, not compassion."

"Which arm." He shrugged.

"Right." She said and flicked the end of the needle to get the air out.

Oliver rolled up his sleeve. "Make it quick, I'm not a fan of needles."

Ellie smiled. "Think about something nice."

"I'll be picturing your smile."

"Oliver." She scowled and stabbed the needle in his arm.

He grimaced but didn't make a sound, exhaling in relief when she pulled the needle from his flesh. "Is that it?"

"Yes." She grinned.

"Try not to look so much like you enjoyed that, Nurse."

"Who says I didn't, Constable?"

He smirked at her. "Fair enough, now lead the way, Princess."

She took a deep breath and squinted at him. "You'll keep. With God's help, we can do this." She smiled and marched out of the room with Oliver on her heels.

*　　*　　*　　*

"What do you suggest, Constable?" The Mayor led the questions.

"I'll let Ellie explain it to you, she knows better than me." He gave her an encouraging smile.

Ellie scowled at him and felt her heckles rise.

Oliver lifted his brows and whispered "Truce" and she nodded and looked at the men before her and Sara who'd been included in the conversation.

"I'll be quick, but I need all of you to help. We've administered the vaccine to all of you who haven't been vaccinated, there are of course no guarantees and I hate to ask you to help when the risk is so high..."

Oliver stopped her briefly. "If any of you wants to leave, you are free to do so, go be with your family, we will ask no more of you. I want no one here who doesn't want to be."

"I'm staying, my students need me," Sara declared. Every member of the council and the reverend nodded their agreement.

Oliver gestured to Ellie again.

"We need to go home to home, I'll teach you how to administer the vaccine. It's not ideal and I shouldn't be asking that of you but with the weather and the people so spread out this is the only way I can think to get the job done, urgently. Start with the children, they're the most vulnerable. Let me know of anyone who has symptoms. I've written the directions out for you and what they should do if they have symptoms, what they can do to help themselves, and quarantine at home.

"Please explain the paramount importance of staying home, even over Christmas. The less movement the less this will spread and the more hope we have of minimizing deaths. I'll try to get to each home where there are sick every day but there is only one of me.

"I warn you, this is a scary and heartbreaking disease and there will be deaths, many of them. We have to be prepared for that."

Oliver raised his brows. "I think we should all go in pairs, we'll meet here every morning and regroup."

"How long will this take?" The reverend asked.

"I can't say. Some weeks – we need to be pox-free for five days before we can declare the epidemic over."

"Hopefully just in time for Christmas," Mr. Cox suggested.

"I can't say, Mr. Cox. Possibly I suppose. Winter doesn't help."

"Alright, let's get started." The Mountie suggested. "You've got your areas of town, we'll regroup here tonight. All information must come through Ellie and me, we don't want to double-handle things. Record any supplies, groceries, or firewood anyone needs and I'll see to it."

"Before we step out, I think I should pray," Robert suggested.

Oliver nodded and everyone stood in a circle while he prayed, and committed the town and the epidemic to the Lord.

Fifteen

"It's been eighteen days, Nurse." The Mayor's voice sounded exhausted and defeated. "Thirteen dead."

Ellie's lips trembled. "I know, I'm sorry for your losses. It's just devastating."

Oliver took the liberty of putting his arm around her. She frowned slightly but gave him a brave smile. He released her and stood back.

"We have three more people sick who are past the worst and on their way to recovery, praise God. I can check in on them."

"We've prepared the bodies for burial and laid them in the vault until the ground thaws." The pastor squeezed Sara's hand, drawing strength from her.

Oliver nodded, he'd recorded all the deaths as per protocol. Two expectant mothers and their babies were among the number. He shuddered. *Another good reason to never marry.*

"You all know what you have to do," Ellie determined to remain stoic, it was her job, but she was exhausted and on the brink of collapse. "We'll meet again in the morning."

"Christmas Eve." Robert grimaced.

"It's going to be a very sad Christmas for the town." Oliver's voice was full of compassion. "The people need all the hope they can get at the moment."

Sara smiled. "Miss Jayne has made Christmas pies, cookies, and candy, could we deliver some in the morning, just spread some joy?"

"Good idea." Oliver cast his eyes to the windows. "But, I believe there is a blizzard coming. We won't go out in the blizzard, it's too dangerous."

"I can't leave the people stranded?" Ellie grimaced.

Oliver turned and gripped her arm. "Ellie, everyone is okay, they have food and wood, and their families, and those who are still sick are on the mend. We need you to be well. Please, promise me you won't go out there if the weather deteriorates."

She looked at him and nodded.

* * * *

A loud banging on the clinic door woke Ellie. She sat up from her chair and looked around. Mrs. Thomas and her son remained in the recovery room, her husband and older son in the next-door room asleep. Peter was over the worst and on his way to recovery. Ellie stood up as the banging increased, straightened her skirts, and headed for the door. Yanking it open she grimaced. "Mr. Harris?"

"Please come, it's Abigail, she's taken a turn for the worse."

Ellie looked around at the weather, for now at least the blizzard had stopped. His horse and sleigh sat out front. She nodded. "Just let me grab my bag."

He nodded and stepped back. Ellie snatched her things and scribbled a hasty note, then ran for the door. Mr. Harris helped her up into the sleigh and they hurried away.

*   *   *   *

"Constable," Mr. Cox greeted him as he strode into the church the next morning.

Oliver looked around and frowned. "Where's Ellie?"

Sara shrugged. "She hasn't arrived yet."

"I know she was really tired. I'll go see if she is still sleeping." Oliver stated. "Please don't go out today. This blizzard is building and it's going to be a bad one. I know it's Christmas. You wanted to deliver treats but it's not worth it. Let's wait out the storm and we can check on the people afterwards. There's no point in you all getting injured or dying, then we are no good to the town. Go on back to your families and I'll check on Ellie. Please be careful going back through the snow. If you go now, while it's eased you'll be fine, you all live close by."

"Thank you, Constable, we'll see to it."

Oliver nodded to the reverend, hurried out, and trudged through the snow to the infirmary. He didn't bother knocking, just walked right in. Ellie had slept in her chair for the previous three weeks of the epidemic, but she wasn't there. "Ellie?" he called, hurrying to check the recovery rooms. He paused as a note on her desk caught his eye.

Gone to Harris Homestead, Abigail has taken a turn.
E

Oliver snatched the paper and wadded it up in his hand clenching his fists tightly. "I told her not to go out there." He shook his head. "Lord, please keep her safe." The fear that rose in him caught him by surprise. "We need her," he admitted out loud. "I need her."

He exhaled loudly and hurried to his office, grabbed his snowshoes and wrapped an extra coat around his shoulders. "I promise I'll find you, Ellie."

Oliver was a gifted tracker, but the snow made it much harder, still, he trudged on in the direction of the Harris homestead. It was only a few miles out of town but as the snow swirled he became disoriented. "Twin pines." He gestured to two trees that were normally positioned at the fork in the road, but the road was buried under several feet of snow. At least it told him he was in the right direction. One more hill and he'd be there.

A groan caught his attention and he peered through the swirling snow. "Hello?" he called but his voice was stolen by the howling wind. He pushed forward, fighting the snow. The groan came again, it was more like a whimper. How he'd heard it was beyond him. It sounded like a wounded animal. He shrugged, he didn't have time for that right now.

Peering through the snow, something caught his eye, it looked like a staggering figure. "What?" He tried to look past the snow drifts. Yes, it was definitely a person. He pushed towards the figure, dismayed to see it was a woman. She staggered along, stumbling and whimpering. She looked up and saw the outline of the Mountie, gasped, and collapsed to the ground.

Oliver grimaced and pushed forward, finally reaching her. He scooped her up and held her close to his chest, thinking quickly where the nearest shelter was. "The Walters Cabin." The Walters had headed West the previous spring and their cabin lay abandoned. "Hold on." He turned to find the twin pines. Barely able to make them out through the storm he sighed in relief, got his bearings, and headed due east.

The woman groaned and moved, the scarf lowered from her face and he gasped. "Ellie?" He hastened his steps, praying the Lord would guide him. If he was out much longer, he was going to freeze to death.

At last the outline of the Walter cabin came into view. "Praise the Lord," he exclaimed as he finally stepped into the cabin and out of the storm.

He lay Ellie on the small sofa before the fireplace and set about making a fire.

*   *   *   *

Ellie opened her eyes and looked around. She frowned. She was in a small cabin, and a warm fire lit the room. She was wrapped in blankets and as her disoriented brain cleared up she frowned again. "Where am I?" She noticed the Mountie seated on the floor leaning against the hearth, a discarded coffee cup sat beside him.

He looked up and smiled. "You're up?"

"Where are we?"

"The old Walters cabin, not far from Twin Pines. I found you in the snow." He knelt before her. "How are you feeling?"

"Really hot."

"I'll remove a few layers." He smiled.

The doors and windows rattled and Ellie's eyes widened. "Wow, that's quite a storm."

"Yes, and I told you not to go out in the storm."

"It was gently falling snow when I left, the Harris homestead." She shrugged.

"Ellie, you know as well as I do that a storm can change quickly, whatever possessed you to go out there?"

"Mr. Harris came to me in the night. I wasn't about to say no."

He smiled. "You are so stubborn..." he raised his brows. "About the most headstrong woman I know."

She shrugged. "Uncle Andrew always said that was a good thing, meant I was determined and wouldn't let anything get in the way of me helping people."

"I never said it was a bad thing."

Ignoring his compliment she changed the subject. "Do you have any more coffee?"

Oliver nodded toward the stove in the small kitchen. "I'll get you some."

"No need. I'm quite able to get coffee."

"I'm happy to." He stood up.

Ellie jumped up from the sofa. "I'm headstrong remember? I can't sit around doing nothing."

"Have it your way." He gestured to the stove. "There's no point trying to argue with you, I know that for sure."

Ellie poured her coffee and twisted up her lips at him. "Then why do you keep trying?"

He shrugged. "A glutton for punishment I suppose."

Ellie merely nodded.

"So how was Abigail anyway?"

Ellie walked back to him and sipped at her cup. "When I got there she was already dead."

Oliver closed his eyes and gripped her arm. "I'm sorry."

"There was no more use for me there, so when the snow subsided, I left them. They didn't need me getting in the way of their grief, mourning their only daughter."

"You should've stayed. You would've been safe."

"I'm safe here aren't I?"

He raised his brows. "You wouldn't be if I hadn't found you."

"Well, rescuing damsels in distress seems to be your forte."

"I was told in no uncertain terms that you are not a damsel in distress."

Ellie opened her mouth to say something but an almighty crack stole her thoughts. "What?" she shrugged. The sound of a tree falling penetrated the night air, Oliver reacted quickly, grabbing her and pulling her out of the way as a branch crashed through the window and missed them by inches. She stood in his arms and both chests heaved as they stared at the branch. Oliver turned to look at her. Ellie's eyes were wide and she was heaving in heavy breaths.

"Are you alright?" he asked as snow and rain swirled in through the broken glass.

She merely nodded.

"I gotta seal this up, or we'll freeze to death." A gust of wind blew the fire out. "You tend the fire."

He sped into action, opening cupboards and looking for what he needed. Ellie yanked the branch into the house and snapped off the smaller sticks stacking them for firewood.

Oliver yanked as hard as he could and pulled the door off the armoire. Opening a cupboard in the kitchen, he was pleased to find a hammer and some nails. Running over he removed the rest of the tree branch and nailed the door over the hole. It didn't completely keep out the snow and cold but it was better.

"The headboard," Ellie suggested, gesturing to the small patch of hole in the window still not covered.

"Good idea, help me?" He asked urgency in his voice. Working together, they dragged it from the bed and broke off a single plank, nailing it over the remaining hole, at last resealing the cabin from the storm.

Ellie looked at him and managed a wry smile.

He turned to her. "Are you alright?"

She smiled. "Yes. I will be when we get this cleaned up. There's glass everywhere." She shivered.

"I'll stoke up the fire," he offered, gesturing to the small pile of sticks she had gathered.

Ellie ran to a cupboard in the kitchen and found a broom, sweeping up the debris into a pile in the corner until she was at last satisfied. She leaned the broom up against the wall and gestured to the hole. "Good fix. It's pretty solid."

"It should hold, provided no more branches come through it."

She nodded and looked at him, suddenly overwhelmed her lip began to tremble.

Oliver frowned and approached her. "Ellie?" He put his hands on her elbows.

Try as she might she couldn't keep the tears at bay. He put his arms out and pulled her close. She shook as she cried out all the emotion from the past few weeks. Laying his chin on her head he said nothing but he couldn't keep his own swirling feelings at bay.

At last, she stood back from him. "Great, you must really think I'm a princess now."

He looked up at her and his eyes shone. "Absolutely."

She scowled at him, "What happened to our Christmas Truce?" She thrust her hands on her hips.

"I haven't broken that."

"But you said you think I'm a princess."

He lifted a hand and tucked some hair behind her ear. "A beautiful princess."

She frowned and stepped back from him. "What are you doing?"

"Saying what I think."

"Which is that you despise me."

He turned his back and stared into the fire, searching his soul for a time. She stood watching him and at last, he turned to look at her. "I don't despise you, Ellie, I admire you actually."

Her brows flew up. "We'll you've certainly got a funny way of showing that. You've made it very clear since I met you that you despise me."

Oliver nodded. "I know. I've gone about this all wrong." He stepped towards her. "It was never you I despised, just your kind."

"My kind?" She crossed her arms.

"Rich people. Truth is my mother used to be a maid in a manor house, the people who lived there were wealthy beyond imagination and they were cruel and vicious, they treated us as little better than slaves and Ma struggled with four children on her own after my father left."

"So that makes all rich people like that?"

He shrugged. "All the ones I've met."

She sighed loudly. "Well, you've got it all wrong. I'm not even rich."

He frowned and raised his brows.

"I was, but when I came here my father disowned me. I have my savings but once that's gone I'll just have what I earn from my clinic."

"He disowned you?"

Ellie's lip trembled. "He was embarrassed by my ambition. It was Uncle Andrew who helped me get here."

"That takes a real toughness, coming here on your own, knowing that you didn't have your father's money to fall back on."

"Was that an apology, Constable?" She put her hands on her hips and tipped her head, fixing her eyes on his, a slight quiver of humor on her lips.

He smiled and stepped forward. "Yes, it's an apology. You have most definitely proven me wrong. I've watched you through this epidemic, you've given everything to the people here at a huge cost to yourself, and you've barely eaten or slept. I've seldom seen such dedication. You have me all tied up in knots because everything inside me wants to despise you because of who you are, or at least were, but the rest wants to... well..." he paused.

"To what, Constable?"

He grinned. "To make the truce permanent?"

Ellie scrunched up her nose and twisted her lips from side to side. "What are you saying? I'm not a princess after all?"

"Oh, you are most definitely a princess." He stroked her cheek. "A very beautiful princess." He looked into her eyes. "I nearly passed out when I saw you at the dance."

"Me?"

"You were wearing that creamy-colored dress with that crown thing on your head and I realized you really were a princess." He dared to lean in and whisper, "and in that moment I wished I was your prince."

She gasped and stepped away from him. "What are you saying?"

He stepped back towards her, cupped her cheek, and dared to lean in and kiss her gently, prolonging it for a time. She closed her eyes and the world began to swirl. Her heart raced and she felt like she was flying. All too soon he pulled back from her. She gasped and stepped away.

"I'm sorry. I shouldn't have done that." Oliver grimaced.

Ellie scowled. "No, you shouldn't have." She raised her hand without thinking and slapped him as hard as she could.

He stepped back and put a hand to his cheek. "What was that for?"

"Taking advantage of our truce."

"What?" He rubbed his cheek, red fingermarks beginning to show. "How did I do that?"

"It's not okay to kiss a woman you don't love."

"Why do you assume I don't love you?"

"You've made it clear you aren't interested in a wife or a family. I'm not interested in being someone you can toy with for your own amusement."

"I'd never do that."

"What about your letters home?"

"Trying to justify my denial." He shook his head and grimaced at her.

"Denial?" She sounded frustrated.

He stepped towards her, lifting a hand to her cheek, he held her eyes with his. "I'd sure like to be your prince."

Ellie tucked her lips under and her eyes flooded with tears.

He stroked her cheek with his thumb. "I think I've loved you from the beginning. I was just so determined to deny it that I couldn't let myself admit it."

"Why not?" Her eyes shone.

"Because love can be excruciating. I saw how much my mother loved my father, and he left her heartbroken. I guess I was scared to love in case I got hurt. A woman like you, so passionate and strong, I feared could never love a man like me. I feel so weak and incapable when I'm around you. It's why I always had to try to prove my strength and your weakness." He chuckled. "It was pathetic, I'm sorry." He brushed her cheek again and his eyes begged hers. "Will you forgive me?"

Ellie looked down at her feet. Oliver removed his hand and sighed. His heart beginning to ache.

"Or am I too late?"

Ellie exhaled loudly, took a deep breath, and stepped forward. She threw her arms around his neck and kissed him.

Oliver gasped and broke the kiss, he looked into her eyes hoping to see the love he hoped for. She smiled and her eyes glistened.

"I take it I'm forgiven." He smiled.

"If you'll forgive me?"

"Of course, there's nothing to forgive, Princess." He winked at her.

"Handsome prince." She grinned at him.

Oliver leaned in and kissed her again, they held the kiss for a time and then both abruptly pulled apart to look toward the window. The storm had stopped as quickly as it had started.

"The storm has stopped." He smiled.

"We should get back. I need to restock for tomorrow."

"Hey, what's your hurry? It's the middle of the night." He glanced up at the clock. "It's after midnight."

"Merry Christmas." She smiled at him.

"The very merriest." He grinned. Something occurred to him and he reached into his pocket. "I have a present for you."

"What?" She frowned.

He pulled his hand out and passed her a small silver broach, it was shaped like a crown decorated with stars and stones of different colors.

"Why do you have that?"

"It was my mother's, she gave it to me and told me I needed to give it to you someday. Her grandfather gave it to her grandmother on their wedding day. He always called his wife 'his princess' and it was her crown. She referred to him as the crown prince of her heart." He winked at her. "Ma thought it appropriate since I referred to you as the princess in my letters. It seems she knew I loved you before I cared to admit it. I argued with her and gave the broach back and after she left I found it in my drawer in my office with a note saying, 'You'll know when to give this to your princess.' I was angry and meant to post it back to her, that's why it's in my coat pocket. I was on my way to post it back when you came storming into my office to tell me about the smallpox. I forgot it was there, until now."

She ran her fingers over it in his hand. "It's so beautiful, how it catches the light."

"Not nearly as beautiful as you, Princess." He smiled and handed it to her.

She took it and pinned it on. "Thank you," she said. "I love it." She raised a hand to his cheek. "Prince of my heart."

He winked and kissed her again. "So, permanent truce?"

She smiled back and grinned. "Yes, of course."

"Now come on, we need to get back to town, we have Christmas cheer to deliver." Oliver grinned.

"What are you saying?"

"Now that the epidemic has subsided and the final few people are recovering, let's deliver those candies and cookies and pies. Let's bring some joy to these people amidst the sadness."

"Sounds wonderful." She smiled.

He reached for her hand. "Come on."

She smiled, snatched up her small bag, and let him lead her out the door.

Sixteen

"Praise the Lord, we're smallpox free." Ellie grinned.

Oliver winked at her from the back of the room. They'd kept their newfound love secret from the others. The town still needed them and it wasn't the right time.

"Praise the Lord, indeed." Robert smiled. "Shall I?"

All heads nodded and he led the gathered congregation in a heartfelt prayer, committing the sorrowing families to the Lord and praying for restoration and healing as the new year approached.

After his amen, Sara stood and addressed the crowd. "Our Christmas pageant never happened this year, but the children and I would like to propose we hold a New Year's Celebration. It could be a memorial for those we lost, as well as a chance to start afresh."

"Wonderful idea." Robert smiled and looked at the people. "All in favor?"

Unanimously the crowd said 'Aye'. The grieving families need to find a reason to smile again.

"Alright, everyone bring what you have and we'll share a meal at my café." Miss Jayne offered.

"I'll donate the fireworks," the store owner, Mr. Hobbes, contributed.

"And we'll see the new year in to make them proud." Mrs. Cunningham had lost two of her children. She brushed away a tear and gripped her husband's hand.

"Very good. Tomorrow night at eight. Providing the weather remains clear."

*   *   *   *

Oliver slipped his arm around Ellie's waist as they stood looking up at the fireworks. Ellie lay her head back against his chest and smiled.

Robert looked across and smiled. He nudged Sara. "Look at that."

She gasped and grinned at him. "Do you think they've finally admitted they love each other?"

"I hope so."

"Took them long enough." She shook her head. "It was obvious."

"Let's go find out," the reverend suggested. Sidling up to the couple he smiled. "Hello, you two."

Ellie and Oliver instinctively stepped away from each other. The semi-darkness hid their glowing cheeks.

Robert raised his brows. "I'm pleased for the two of you."

Oliver grinned sheepishly and gripped Ellie's hand. "You don't seem surprised."

"We knew you loved each other, known it from the start."

"Really?" Ellie asked.

Sara chuckled. "Sparks like you two had usually turn into fireworks eventually."

"I'm sorry it took me so long to see it." Ellie grimaced.

"I didn't make it easy for you." Oliver squeezed her hand.

"It's alright, I'm glad we've declared a truce." Ellie grinned. "That's what led to all this."

"Ah, the Christmas Truce. We'll never forget that." Oliver smiled. "Christmas was always my least favorite time of year and now it's my favorite.

"Mine too." Ellie smiled. "But you know what's better?"

"What?"

"The New Year's Truce?"

"New Year's Truce?" Oliver questioned.

"We declared war on the smallpox. We lost a few people along the way but now we've called a truce on that war. We get to start the new year afresh. It's wonderful."

"Yes, it is." Robert nodded.

At that moment the mayor yelled out, "Ten seconds to midnight."

"Nine, eight, seven, six, five..." the town chanted together. "Four, three, two, one. Happy New Year." The shout was accompanied by a skyrocket exploding right on cue.

A voice began to sing 'Lest auld acquaintance be forgot..." All the voices around lifted to accompany the singer.

Oliver looked at Ellie and stroked her face. They shared a brief kiss and then leaned their heads together to watch the fireworks while the people continued to sing. They smiled as the snow lit up with colors and lights. A town in mourning looking forward with hope to the upcoming year.

"Happy New Year, Princess." Oliver grinned at her.

"Happy New Year, Prince of my heart." She returned his grin.

The end.

About the Author

Jo Dawson grew up on a dairy farm in Wellsford, a small town in the North Island of New Zealand. She spent fifteen years as a teacher in New Zealand and abroad, before becoming a stay-at-home mum and completing her graduate degree in Theology.

She has lived in Australia and the USA for a time, and these experiences have added to her love of people and history. Blessed with a vivid imagination and the love of classical literature and historical fiction, Jo virtually grew up best friends with Anne Shirley, romping with Jo March and her sisters, sailing a raft down the Mississippi with Huckleberry Finn or living in the 'little house' with Laura Ingalls.

Born and raised in a strong Christian family, Jo's faith is at the centre of who she is, with a lifetime of being involved in churches and Christian camps. These two loves, literature and the Lord, have inevitably converged into writing compelling stories of strong Christian women, courageously facing the hardships of life on the frontier. It is her hope that women of all ages would find encouragement from her heroines' experiences that, while fiction, so often mirror even our modern lives.

Jo currently resides in the small North Island town of Waipu in New Zealand, where she lives with her husband, and a very lazy cat.

<u>Other books by J. L. Dawson</u>

Journeys of the Heart Series
Awakening of the Heart
Shepherd of the Heart
Decisions of the Heart
A Home for the Heart
Blessings of the Heart
Legacies of the Heart

Douglas Falls Series
Prequel: The Cost of Duty
A Duty to Love
Twixt Duty and Love
A Duty to Family
The Duty of a Father
A Duty to Serve.

Multiple Author Series (Standalone books).
Hers to Redeem Book 14: Aaron's Anguish
Hers to Redeem Book 18: Mitchell's Misfortune
Hers to Redeem Book 21: Robbie's Roaming
Hers to Redeem Book 22: Rueben's Risk
Winning His Devotion, Book 8: Ezra's Duty
Second Chance Groom Book 9: Romancing the Attorney
Double Trouble Book 10: Jacob's Brides
Double Trouble Book 14: Andy' Brides
Sleigh Ride Book 5: A Sleigh Ride For Aven.
The Matchmaker and the Mother-in-law Book 15: Molly's wedding Dilemma
Wear Hearts and Wounded Spirits Book 11: Hearts at Stake

Standalone Books
To Love Nate – A Companion to Aaron's Anguish.

<u>Where to find these books:</u>
https://www.amazon.com/stores/J-L-Dawson/author
www.jodawsonauthor.com to sign up for my newsletter
jldawsonauthor@yahoo.com to write to the author
Jo Dawson and **J. L. Dawson Author**
-on Instagram and Facebook